WARHAMMER™
ADVENTURES
STORIES IN AN AGE OF FANTASY

# FLIGHT OF THE KHARADRON

TOM HUDDLESTON

WARHAMMER ADVENTURES

First published in Great Britain in 2020 by
Warhammer Publishing,
Willow Road,
Nottingham, NG7 2WS, UK.

10 9 8 7 6 5 4 3 2 1

Produced by Games Workshop in Nottingham.
Cover illustration by Cole Marchetti.
Internal illustrations by Dan Boultwood & Cole Marchetti.



A CIP record for this book is available from the British Library.

ISBN 13: 978 1 78193 965 9



See Warhammer Adventures on the internet at

**warhammeradventures.com**

Find out more about Games Workshop and the worlds of Warhammer 40,000 and Warhammer Age of Sigmar at

**games-workshop.com**

Printed and bound by CPI Group (UK) Ltd, Croydon, CR0 4YY

REALM QUEST
OF THE

Book 1 CITY OF LIFESTONE

Book 2 LAIR OF THE SKAVEN

Book 3 FOREST OF THE ANCIENTS

Book 4 FLIGHT OF THE KHARADRON

Book 5 FORTRESS OF GHOSTS (November 2020)

WARPED GALAXIES

Book 1 ATTACK OF THE NECRON

Book 2 CLAWS OF THE GENESTEALER

Book 3 SECRETS OF THE TAU

Book 4 WAR OF THE ORKS

Book 5 PLAGUE OF THE NURGLINGS (November 2020)

# Contents

# The Mortal Realms

Each of the Mortal Realms is a world unto itself, steeped in powerful magic. Seemingly infinite in size, there are endless possibilities for discovery and adventure: floating cities and enchanted woodlands, noble beings and dread beasts beyond imagination. But in every corner of the realms, battles rage between the armies of Order and the forces of Chaos. This centuries-long war must be won if the realms are to live in peace and freedom.

PROLOGUE

# Seven months ago…

The big man crouched beneath the awning of the apothecary's stall, fixing Alish with a hard stare. His name was Crusher and his red cloak marked him as a member of the Scarlet Shadow, the most feared gang in the city of Lifestone. He had a sword on his belt, a knife in his boot and a wart on his nose the size of a fist. Alish couldn't stop staring at it.

'Now listen,' he said, scratching his nose self-consciously. 'You stay right here. I'm off to buy the big man a tusker steak for his supper, and I don't want you getting any ideas.'

'I wouldn't,' Alish said, still transfixed by the wart. 'Get any, I mean. Ideas.'

She was telling the truth – she had no plans to run away. The Shadow might be a pack of brutes, but at least with them she got food and shelter and protection. She didn't have to live on the streets like the other orphans she'd seen hanging around.

Crusher marched away through the quiet market and Alish turned back to the stall, inspecting the goods on offer. There was bloodmoss from the swamps of Quogmia and bladeroot from the haunted forests beyond the Everlight River. There were caskets of quick spice from the city of Hammerhal, and even a small jar of blackpowder that the storekeeper claimed came all the way from Chamon, the Realm of Metal. Alish wanted badly to buy it, but she knew her masters would never allow it. The Scarlet Shadow gave her a certain amount of independence to pick the materials she needed for her inventions, but there were limits to how much she could spend. Still, she could only imagine the bang it would make.

A shadow fell over her. Had Crusher returned already? But when she turned she saw another man standing there, older, taller and much thinner. He wore a broad-brimmed black hat and a long cloak, and there were two children with him – a muscular, red-haired girl and a short, shifty-looking boy, lurking in the shadows.

'Hello, Alish,' the man said, and his eyes twinkled. 'My name is Vertigan. We'd like to talk to you.'

As the children stared at her, Alish felt a strange tingling in her wrist. She tugged her sleeve down, hiding the black mark on her skin. She'd heard all the rumours about this old man – folks called him the Shadowcaster; they said he bewitched people and carried them away to the Arbour, that old ruined palace on the hill.

‘Leave me alone,’ she said. ‘I don’t know you, and you don’t know me.’

‘I know more than you think,’ he said. ‘I know your name, and I know that on your wrist you bear the mark of Hysh, the Realm of Light. I know you live with the gang who did away with your parents, I know they use you to make weapons for them and I know it’s a terrible waste of your talents. You should be helping people, Alish, not hurting them.’

‘I never hurt anyone,’ she said defensively. ‘What the Shadow choose to do with the things I make is their choice, not mine.’

Vertigan sighed. ‘If that’s what you tell yourself, I don’t blame you for it. But you can’t hide from the truth forever, Alish. You need to face your responsibilities. You need to see the damage you’re doing. We can help you find your true purpose.’

She turned her back. ‘Get away,’ she said. ‘You don’t know what my life’s like, you don't get to say what I should do. I'll make my own decisions, thank you very m–'

'Who are you talking to?'

Alish spun round in surprise. Crusher stood over her, frowning. He had a tusker steak over one shoulder and he'd smeared some sort of pinkish substance on his nose – she suspected it was meant to disguise the wart, but all it did was make it stand out.

But there was no sign of the Shadowcaster, or the children. They'd vanished into the crowd.

Alish shrugged. 'Talking to myself, I suppose.'

Her workshop was tucked away in the third basement of the gang's hideout, a disused storehouse in the old industrial quarter of the city. Most of the buildings here were abandoned – Lifestone had once been a thriving place, she'd heard, but those times were long gone. The only ones making any money nowadays were rat-catchers, funeral parlours and criminals like the Scarlet Shadow.

She studied the crossbow she'd been working on, holding it up in the flickering lantern light. If she could just find a way to trim a little bit of extra weight, it might be possible to fire it one-handed. Now that would make her masters happy.

She could hear a group of them in the armoury above, their boots clumping on the boards. They were getting ready for a mission – she'd heard Crusher and one of the others discussing it as they locked her in after the trip to the market. They would come back late at night, rowdy and raucous, and she'd lie awake wondering what awful things they'd done with the weapons she'd crafted.

She thought of the old man in the market, his words echoing in her head. *Face your responsibilities... See the damage you're doing.* Suddenly, she made a decision.

Getting out of her room wasn't difficult; there was a loose board in the wall, she'd done it countless times. She stole up the stairway just as the gang were leaving, twelve of them striding out into the night. The moon was high so Alish had no trouble following them, slipping from shadow to shadow along the silent street. It helped that the men made quite a racket, laughing and bickering, strapping on their armour as they walked.

But as they left the narrow streets of

the lower city and moved up into the tradesman's district, the group began to fall silent. Alish dropped back, creeping on tiptoes as they crossed a wide street lined with bare trees, entering a courtyard with a temple on the near side, a huge bronze hammer standing in front of it like a statue.

Suddenly she knew where they were going. Across the square she could see a high, curved wall, the base lined with stone arches. Beside every arch was a stone figure, chiselled in the likeness of a warrior who had fought and died in the now derelict arena.

The gang ducked into one of the arches and Alish followed, slipping along a brick-lined tunnel. It forked and she listened for their footsteps, taking the right-hand way. Soon she could hear voices, and she crept into the open, holding her breath.

The bowl-shaped arena brimmed with shadows. Stone benches rose steeply on either side, scattered with fallen statues and masonry. The combat floor was entirely dark, but squinting ahead Alish could see figures waiting on the sand, their pack animals snorting in the night-time cold. The men moved towards them, and Alish heard a shout of greeting.

She slid closer, ducking behind the benches. She could hear them clearly – Crusher and a gruff-voiced man. No, not a man – a Duardin, one of the dwarf-folk. His fellows hung back; ten or twelve stocky, thickly bearded figures, four mules and a pair of rickety carts piled high with goods.

'I know we agreed eighty,' Crusher was saying, 'but things are different now. Fifty's the best we can do.'

The Duardin snorted. 'But that's robbery. This is flawless craftsmanship, some of these pieces have been in our family for generations. We're leaving Lifestone, there's no way to make a decent living here any more. And we need that money if we're going to get to Hammerhal. I won't have my youngbeards starve on the road.'

Crusher shrugged. 'No need for the sob story. We've made our offer, take it or leave it.'

The Duardin growled. 'Where's Stonejaw? He's the one who made this bargain.'

'He's busy,' Crusher told him. 'But he gave me strict instructions not to go above fifty.'

'Well then the deal's off,' the Duardin said bitterly. 'I'll find another buyer, even if it means staying longer. What you're offering is an insult to me and my people.'

Crusher scratched his wart. 'You don't seem to understand. We're leaving with the goods, that's happening. You can either take the fifty, or nothing at all.'

The Duardin took a step back. '*Oathbreaker*,' he hissed, like a curse. Then he turned, waving at his companions. 'We've been cheated! It's a tr–'

The crossbow bolt struck him in the shoulder and the Duardin staggered into the sand. Alish clapped a hand over her mouth. The bolt was lightweight and steel-tipped, fletched with goshawk feathers. One of hers.

She saw the other Duardin ducking behind their carts as more bolts thudded into the wood, the mules whinnying in panic. The gang drew their swords, marching forward with murder in their eyes. Alish crouched lower, her heart pounding. So it was true. The Scarlet Shadow didn't just rob people, or trick them, or scare them. They killed them.

Arrows rained down around the advancing men and Alish heard one of them cry out as a massive metal hammer spiralled through the air, glancing off his armour and thundering into the dust. It skidded towards Alish and lay still.

Instinctively she reached for it, hefting it in her hand. The Duardin had spoken truthfully – this was fine craftsmanship. The head was solid but light, the shaft perfectly designed for gripping. She clutched it as she backed away, turning her back on the fighting.

Then she heard footsteps behind her, and ducked aside as a small figure hurtled past, weaving in terror. It was a Duardin child, barely up to her shoulder, with a wispy beard and fear in his eyes. She'd seen that fear before – no, she'd *felt* it, the night that her parents disappeared and the Shadow took her. The boy sprinted on, making for the nearest tunnel and vanishing inside.

'He got away!' a man shouted. 'He went in there!'

'I'll go after him,' Crusher replied. 'You keep the others pinned down.'

Alish saw him stride past, sword in hand. The boy might lose him, if he was lucky. But what if he wasn't? Gripping the hammer, she got to her feet. The tunnel was a dark mouth, opening before her. Swallowing her fear she stepped inside.

She could hear Crusher up ahead, calling to the boy.

'Don't run, little beardling. I'm going to take you to your daddy.' Then in a low voice he muttered, 'Nothing like a good hostage to make a stubborn Duardin put his sword down.'

Alish hurried after them, turning left then right, beginning to lose her bearings. The darkness was absolute, the walls closing in. She felt her heart pound, and wondered what in Sigmar's name she was doing.

Then she heard a laugh, and her blood ran cold.

'There you are,' Crusher said. 'Now just get over here, and– aaagh! You little rat!'

Alish hugged the wall, peering into an empty hall. The ceiling was cracked and shafts of moonlight fell, illuminating two figures. Crusher had two fingers in his mouth, his face flushed with anger.

The Duardin boy crouched a short distance away, blood on his lips and terror in his eyes.

Crusher strode forward, hands outstretched. But as he passed the opening where Alish crouched she sprang from the shadows, shoving him off his feet. She grabbed the trembling youngbeard, pointing to the far side of the hall where an archway stood open. Through it she could see the Duardin temple.

'Go,' she hissed. 'Find your people. Stay safe.'

The boy fled, out into the night. Crusher picked himself up. His eyes widened.

'You!'

Alish nodded, hefting the hammer. 'Me.'

Crusher reached over his shoulder, yanking something from a harness on his back. Alish recognised it – a crossbow, one of hers, light and deadly. But it was an old model, and it tended to pull to the right.

'You just dug your own grave,' Crusher said, loading an arrow and taking aim. 'And after we fed you, raised you, kept you from harm.'

'You got your money's worth,' Alish said. 'But it ends here.'

His finger squeezed the trigger and she threw herself left as the arrow glanced off the wall. Gripping the hammer, she fled for the nearest tunnel, taking one turning then another, emerging into the courtyard. There was no sign of the Duardin boy, and behind them the din of battle had abated. She wondered which side had won.

Then she heard Crusher coming after her and realised she had nowhere to go. She could flee the city, she supposed – if she stayed, the Shadow would surely find her.

Then her gaze lifted to the slopes above, to the palace on the peak, a sprawl of white buildings gleaming in the moonlight. The Arbour, home of the

Shadowcaster. Well, it was worth a try.

She bolted across the square and into the maze of buildings on the far side, heading uphill. Her legs were weary and her head was ringing – she'd seen too much, done too much, and it was way past her bedtime.

Alish darted from alley to alley, crossed street after street, always heading upwards. She barely knew this part of the city, where the rich folk lived. It wouldn't take much to get completely lost.

She paused for a moment, looking around. Pale buildings rose, blocking the view in all directions. The ground was flat, she wasn't even sure which way was up. And it wouldn't be long before–

'Found you.'

From an alley, a hulking figure appeared. Crusher's face was red with exertion, his wart gleaming in the moonlight. His hand dropped to the sword at his belt.

'You ungrateful guttersnipe. No one

betrays the Scarlet Shadow and lives to... lives to...'

He broke off, frowning. For a moment Alish thought she felt a strange tingling in the air, then a breeze blew and it passed. Crusher had stopped in his tracks, looking at her in confusion. He stared at his sword, then up again.

'Um, who are...' he asked, frowning. 'Wh... where are...'

Alish watched him. Had he suddenly lost his mind, or was he trying to trick her somehow?

Then a voice spoke from the shadows, clear and calm.

'Leave this girl alone,' it said. 'Go back to the hole you crawled out of, and forget she ever existed.'

Crusher frowned, his eyes losing focus. He shrugged. 'Um, okay. If you say so.'

And he turned and ambled away, leaving Alish open-mouthed. She looked for the source of the voice, and as the moon broke from the clouds a figure was revealed, standing on the cobbles with a satisfied expression on his face.

'Well that went surprisingly well, didn't it?' the Shadowcaster said with a smile. 'It always seems to work better with the stupid ones.'

CHAPTER ONE

# Down the Gullet

The sky-beast's mighty jaws snapped shut and Alish clung to the railing as the *Arbour Seed* was swallowed, sluicing from side to side as they raced down the creature's throat. All around them she could hear the thump-thump of the monster's blood, its huge heart pumping.

The flying creature had come upon them in the skies above the city of Lifestone, as Alish was struggling to pilot the airship home. It had hunted them through the clouds, snapping up the *Arbour Seed* and its passengers as they tumbled towards the ground.

Now they were sliding down its gullet, lost in warm, pounding heat.

Thick liquid splashed over the railing and Alish felt a wave of disgust as it clung to her clothes, her skin, her hair. She wiped herself clean but the stench was hideous, rotting meat and bile. They tipped forward and Elio cried out, clutching her hand as the incline grew steeper and they picked up speed, rocketing along the pink, fleshy tunnel.

Alish looked around in confusion. 'Wait,' she said, almost to herself. 'How can I see?'

'This stuff's luminous,' Elio said, wiping a splash of bile from his face. He was right; it was glowing a faint, almost ghostly green, lighting up the pulsating passage.

'It stings, too, if you leave it too long,' Kiri said, mopping her face with her sleeve. 'Try not to get any on you.'

Suddenly a shape loomed from the shadows ahead – a razor-sharp beak and massive spread wings. But the bird was dead, Alish saw, black feathers clinging to rotted bones. It must've been swallowed just like them, and become lodged in the creature's throat. The passage tilted downwards and the airship picked up speed, the wave of bile carrying them past strange openings in the walls of the gullet, like corridors leading deeper into the creature's gut.

'It must have multiple stomachs,' Elio said in wonder. 'I've heard of this, some creatures have these– aaaagh!'

The passage suddenly opened out, and for a moment they were falling, saliva raining around them. There was a giant splash as they landed, dropping into a pool of wet, sticky, faintly glowing warmth. Alish took a breath, trying to calm herself. They were still alive, and that was a good start.

The glow lit up the sides of the gondola, the wrecked balloon overhead and their five damp, startled faces.

'Look on the bright side,' Kaspar said.

'At least we're not going to crash any more.'

Thanis snorted, then shook her head. 'This isn't funny. I don't know what it is yet, but it's definitely not funny.'

'Wait, is there… is there someone over there?' Kiri whispered, pointing.

Alish peered out. In the queasy green light she could see the walls of the chamber, pink and fleshy and veined in blue. There were shapes in the gloom: white bones and furred remains, and the black shell of some vast flying insect. And following Kiri's finger she could indeed see figures in the dark, pale and motionless, staring at them from empty, eyeless sockets.

'Looks like they've been here a while,' Elio whispered. 'What's that contraption they're sitting in?'

It was shaped roughly like their own airship, but slightly larger and constructed from steel instead of wood. The skeletal figures slumped inside, armoured in bronze and leather, had

wispy beards still clinging to their masked faces.

'They're Kharadron!' Alish realised. 'The Duardin who worked out how to fly. They must have been swallowed too, like we were.'

There was a sudden flash of light and Alish felt the strangest sensation, a sort of tugging in her muscles as though she'd suddenly moved without moving.

'What was that?' Thanis whispered. 'I feel... like I've felt it before.'

'You have,' Kiri said. 'It felt like it did

when we went through the gnawhole into the Skaven tunnels. And like it did when I came through the Realmgate.'

'You mean we're in a different realm?' Kaspar asked. 'How is that possible?'

Elio's eyes lit up. 'I've read about this. There are supposed to be creatures, very rare ones, that can actually move between realms of their own accord. It's like how some fish can travel from the salt sea to fresh water, to lay their eggs. They feed in one realm, and spawn in another.'

Kiri frowned. 'Maybe we'll get lucky and it'll take us to Shyish, so we can find Vertigan.'

Their master had been stolen by a sorceress named Ashnakh, and they still weren't sure why. It had something to do with the birthmarks each of them bore. They'd been on their way back to the besieged city of Lifestone to look for clues when the sky-beast had eaten them.

'Do you have any idea how big

each realm is?' Elio asked. 'Even if we happened to end up in Shyish, the chances of us finding where she's keeping him are–'

'Um, this is all very fascinating,' Thanis said, peering over the side. 'But we've got a bigger problem. Alish, look!'

Alish joined her, looking down. They were floating in a lake of bile with foul bubbles erupting from it, emitting clouds of stinking gas. But there was a darker mist in the air too, hissing from the side of the airship.

'It's dissolving the wood,' she said, fighting to keep the panic from her voice. 'It's like Kiri said, it burns like acid. It's eating the airship!'

Elio wrung his hands. 'Is there anything you can do?'

Alish gulped. 'I didn't really plan for this. I thought we might hit something or fall out of the sky, I didn't think we'd get swallowed by some giant big massive–'

'Hey,' Kiri said. 'Take a breath, and

let's figure out what to do.'

'Well there's only one way out of here,' Thanis said, looking up. The creature's gullet was a pulsating portal overhead, saliva dripping from it.

'Technically there's two,' Kaspar pointed out. 'But I don't really want to try the other route, do you?'

*He's trying to seem calm,* Alish thought, *but deep down he must be as scared as any of us.* Kaspar's hand had slipped inside his shirt and he was touching something restlessly, his fingers wrapped around it. Alish frowned – a few days before, he had come into possession of a pendant, a black pyramid that turned out to have come from the same sorceress that had stolen Vertigan. He said he'd thrown it away, but could he have lied to them?

'Look, the Duardin ship hasn't dissolved,' Kiri was saying. 'The stuff must eat through wood but not steel. If we can get there, it'd at least buy us some time.'

Alish nodded, pulling a screw-loosener from her tool belt, wishing her hands would stop shaking. 'If we detach one of the struts that hold up the boiler pipe we could use it to push ourselves along,' she said. 'The stern-side strut's the longest, if we take out the bolts here and here we should be able to... What's that?'

They froze, listening. The sound seemed to come from all around them, a distant buzzing.

'Listen,' Elio said. 'The heart. I think it's speeding up.'

He was right – the creature's pulse had quickened, pounding through the fleshy walls. The air seemed to grow more stifling, the bubbles in the bile fizzing more rapidly.

'Is it...' Elio asked, confused. 'Is it scared?'

Kiri grinned. 'Maybe something's after it. That'll teach it to go around eating people.'

'But you have to wonder,' Kaspar said.

'What could possibly scare something this big?'

The buzzing grew louder, seeming to circle around them. The beast's heartbeat thudded faster. Then suddenly the entire chamber started to revolve around them, bile splashing over the railings as the creature rolled. Alish leapt back, avoiding a surge of stinging green slime as the *Arbour Seed* tipped then crashed back down, riding the steepening wave. The walls were closing in, the stomach contracting. There was a deep, guttural roar, the creature bellowing. But it was suddenly cut off, muffled somehow, as though the beast had been gagged, though that was surely impossible.

'What's happening?' Thanis cried out as the lake of bile boiled madly.

Elio grabbed the railing. 'Everybody, hang on!'

A geyser erupted beneath them and the *Arbour Seed* was lifted upwards, the walls of the chamber dropping away as they shot towards the ceiling and through the opening in its centre.

Borne on a green wave they were swept back into the gullet, clinging on desperately. They passed the different openings and the lodged skeleton, driven on a crashing wall of thick liquid.

Then suddenly they stopped, waves of bile crashing past them like a fast-flowing river. Alish looked up.

'We're stuck!'

Part of the balloon's support structure

had become wedged in the creature's throat, pinning them in place. The walls throbbed around them, the monster hacking and coughing desperately.

'Can you cut us loose?' Kiri shouted over the din.

Alish crouched by the strut, feeling for the bolts. They were stiff, but she tugged on her screw-loosener and the first one came free, dropping into her hand. The creature coughed again, breath and saliva whooshing past them – it was like trying to work in a gale.

Then the other bolt dropped out and the strut crashed down, leaving an angry purple mark on the roof of the gullet. The sky-beast gave another cough and the *Arbour Seed* was thrown forward. Alish saw light up ahead, the creature's teeth like stalactites in the mouth of a cave.

Then they were free, and falling.

CHAPTER TWO

# The Kharadron

The airship dropped vertically and Alish had visions of them plummeting, falling thousands of metres to shatter on solid rock. But before she could take a breath they'd slammed to a halt, splashing down into a pool of saliva.

She looked around in astonishment. Steel walls rose on every side, a circular container keeping them in. More saliva poured in, splashing around them.

'Are we...' Kaspar asked in amazement. 'Are we in some kind of *bucket*?'

He was right – they were in a metal

pail twice as wide as the *Arbour Seed* and about the same depth. Hearing a mighty cough Alish looked up, shielding her eyes from the glaring silver sky. What she saw took her breath away.

The sky-beast hung overhead, its tail flapping wildly, its huge paws swiping at the air. There were smaller shapes circling it – darting, steel-hulled craft festooned with weapons and rigging. Kharadron frigates, Alish realised, just like the one in the monster's stomach.

From one of the larger vessels a long

pole extended, and at its end was a hoop of metal – a noose. This had been tightened around the creature's neck, holding it in place as it kicked and fought. As they watched, another small airship drifted closer, a huge ram extending from its prow. The ram was coated with material, springy and white like wool. Alish watched in astonishment as the airship floated in, forcing the ram into the creature's mouth.

The sky-beast coughed again, spluttering and bellowing. They covered their heads as more bile rained down.

'They're making it throw up,' Elio said, quickly mopping the stinging slime from his face. 'But why?'

'Maybe they drink it,' Thanis said, and Alish felt ill at the thought.

'Maybe it's got mystical properties,' Kiri suggested.

'Or maybe these Duardin just have a really weird sense of fun,' Kaspar muttered.

The Kharadron ships withdrew and with a roar the sky-beast began to buck, struggling against the noose. Alish could see Duardin on the deck of the largest craft, fighting to unhook it. The noose slipped off and the sky-beast turned, roaring furiously. Then it soared away, its great body undulating as it swept into the clouds and was gone.

Suddenly there was a clunk beneath them and the airship started to drop. Looking over the side Alish could see a hole in the base of the bucket, the sticky liquid draining away. The *Arbour Seed* spun in the whirlpool, but the funnel was too small; they were beached on the bottom along with the battered Kharadron craft, the ragged Duardin skeletons and the feathery remains of the giant bird.

For a moment, all was quiet.

'Do you think they've seen us?' Alish whispered, gesturing to the airships circling overhead. 'Do you think they'll–'

The base of the bucket fell away,

opening like a hatch. They dropped through, but again it was a short fall – Alish had time to let out a short yelp of surprise, then they landed, hard this time, the airship tipping over as they crashed onto a wide steel deck.

She tumbled out, rolling on her back. Above her she could see the huge bucket, suspended on sturdy metal struts, and beside it a bronze tank sloshing with bile. Past that a large black shape was suspended in mid-air, a spherical drum painted with a silver compass, attached to the deck by steel struts. *Is that how they fly?* she wondered.

Then someone groaned, and she sat up. The *Arbour Seed*'s balloon was rags now, the boiler's support structure shredded to pieces. But the gondola was surprisingly intact, considering all it had been through. A few timbers had split and she could see acid burns all along the lower half, but overall it was in one piece. She felt a flush of pride as she tottered to her feet.

Kiri climbed out, the others following. The airship they'd landed on was truly massive, its black steel plates held together with rivets bigger than Alish's head. The deck was wide, and towards the prow she could see a cabin studded with portholes.

'A Kharadron Ironclad,' she said under her breath. 'I never imagined...'

A hatch slammed open in the deck, making them all jump.

'Now then,' a voice barked. 'Let's see what that dirty great monster has given us this time, shall we?'

A figure emerged from the hatch. The first thing Alish saw was an unruly tower of orange hair, followed by a face that seemed to be made of silver. Its eyes were perfect circles, its mouth bright with steel teeth, and even its red moustaches were painted on.

'What in blazes...' a muffled voice said, and Alish realised it was a mask, sculpted to look like a Duardin face.

'Get up here, you lubbers. We've got company!'

The masked figure clambered up, placing a gigantic three-cornered hat on his head. More Duardin followed, streaming from the hatch. They wore silver masks and flight suits with the compass pattern on the breast, and their pockets bulged with wrenches and spanners and flintlock pistols.

The first one strode forward, his hobnail boots clanking on the deck. 'What are you?' he asked, squinting through glass lenses. 'Treasure, or trouble?'

Kiri held up her hands. 'We're neither. We're just simple travellers.'

The Duardin leaned back in surprise. 'You're children,' he said. 'Human children. What in the name of Grungni were you doing in the belly of a wingless realm-rider?'

'It ate us,' Alish said. 'We were in our ship and it gulped us down.'

'If you could drop us back in Lifestone, we'd appreciate it,' Elio added.

The Duardin frowned. 'Lifestone? Is that even in the Silverlands? Doesn't sound like anywhere I've ever heard of, not in this region of Chamon.'

*So that's where we are,* Alish thought. *The Realm of Metal.*

The Duardin raised his goggles onto his head, looking them carefully up and down. Alish got the distinct sense that he was judging their worth. 'Well wherever you came from, you don't look dangerous,' he said, extending a gloved hand. 'Torvald Skysplitter's the name, trader in goods and information, aether-gold and regular gold, anything I can buy cheap and sell pricey. This is my boat, the *Mercury Maid.*' He gestured to the prow, where a silver figurehead rose from the deck – a female figure in flowing robes.

Kiri shook his hand and Alish followed, wincing at the captain's vice-like grip. 'Are all these other craft yours, too?' she managed, working the blood back into her fingers.

Torvald nodded. 'This is my little fleet, seven ships all told. Built 'em up from nothing, I did. But that's a long story.'

'Why were you trying to make that… thing… sick?' Elio asked.

The captain grunted. 'That's our latest venture,' he said without enthusiasm. 'Realm-rider bile is highly prized by mystics and apothecaries. It's messy work, but the money's good. And every so often one of those monsters will bring up something of real value.'

He walked around the *Arbour Seed*, inspecting the gondola.

'This isn't bad,' he said. 'Not up to Kharadron standards, of course, but solid craftsmanship. Where did you find it?'

'We didn't find it,' Alish told him. 'I built it.'

The captain laughed. 'But you're a child.'

Alish flushed. 'I'm an inventor. I designed it and made it, and we all flew in it.'

Torvald appraised her. 'You must be a very bright girl. I don't know if that's a good thing or a bad thing.' He glanced at his fellow Duardin. 'What do you think, boys? Do people want a clever slave, or do they prefer them dumb and dutiful?'

Alish gasped, and Kiri's hand dropped to her catapult.

'You're not selling us,' Thanis said, bunching her gloved fists. 'We're not your property.'

'You fell out of a realm-rider's belly onto my deckplates,' Torvald said, looking up at her. 'I'd say that makes you legitimate salvage.'

'But I thought the Duardin didn't deal in slaves,' Kaspar protested.

'Not officially,' Torvald admitted. 'But we're headed for Barak-Mhornar, the City of Shadow. A lot goes on there that isn't exactly legal. We'll find a buyer for you, don't worry.'

'No,' Kiri said, whipping out her catapult and loading it, aiming it at the captain's head. 'I've been a slave before. I won't be one again.'

Torvald gestured and his men fanned out, circling them silently. Each one was armed, glaring unsympathetically through their goggles.

'You don't have to do this,' Alish pleaded. 'We're worth more as workers than slaves. Thanis here is as strong as a rhinox, and Elio's a healer, he can mend any wound. Kiri's tough and quick, and Kaspar, well, he's sneakier than anyone I ever met. I built that flying machine, I'm sure your mechanics can find a use for me. I even have my own hammer.'

She detached her prized Duardin hammer from the clip on her back, holding it up in the steely sunlight. Torvald inspected it, nodding appreciatively. But still he shook his head.

'No, I'm afraid I can't have five strange men-folk running loose on my ship. Seize their weapons and take them to the brig.'

CHAPTER THREE

# The Sky-city

Alish gazed down through the glass floor as the landscape of Chamon rolled beneath them. Streams of mercury flowed into mirrored lakes, between jagged mountains of iron ore ranged with copper-coloured forests. The clouds drifted by, as dark as gunmetal, raining showers of silver. Sometimes she saw seams of gold sparkling in their depths – the same substance they'd encountered over Lifestone, the stuff that had got into the *Arbour Seed*'s workings and made it rocket up into the sky. She was sure it was what powered the Kharadron's ships.

They'd been in here for a day and a night now, without water or food, just the last of what the Sylvaneth had given them. The *Mercury Maid*'s brig was bolted to the bottom of the ship, a transparent blister facing directly downwards. At first it had been terrifying – Alish was sure it was going to crack, that they were going to plummet to their deaths. But gradually she'd grown accustomed to it. It was amazing, she thought, what a person could get used to.

They'd explored the possibility of breaking out, but without Alish's tools or Kaspar's lock-picking kit it had proved impossible. And as the hours dragged by they fell into silence, Elio shivering pensively, Kaspar pulling his hood over his face. Kiri crouched like a coiled spring, muttering to herself, while Thanis just curled up and started snoring. She could sleep anywhere, Alish knew. It was a talent she envied, especially at times like now, when she was too scared to close her eyes.

But, she admitted to herself, it wasn't just fear that kept her awake. She was fascinated, too – by the new realm in which they found themselves, but most of all by the Ironclad itself. For as long as she could remember she'd wanted to see a real Kharadron airship, and now she was inside one. The question was, how to get out?

There was a clunk overhead and she looked up, shaking Thanis. The brig's hatch lifted and a face peered through – a rusty mask beneath straggly grey hair.

'Captain wants to see you,' the old Duardin said, lowering a ladder.

Kiri frowned. 'What for?'

He shrugged. 'Not my business. Come on, up you get.'

They climbed into a steel corridor, deep in the belly of the airship. Beams creaked and pipes hissed as they followed the ageing Kharadron up a winding stairway. Light filtered through a hatch above, and the walls were dark with rust.

They emerged onto the deck, breathing fresh, metallic air. Ahead of them was the tall cabin and in the doorway stood Torvald Skysplitter, beckoning to them. His face was unmasked to reveal ruddy cheeks and behind him the sun was sinking, a heavy bank of clouds looming on the horizon. In them Alish saw that strange sparkle again, and as they reached the cabin she pointed to it.

'What is that stuff?' she asked. 'Does it make your ships stay up?'

The captain nodded. 'Aye. We call it aether-gold, it's the most marvellous substance there is. We feed it into the endrins, you see, there.'

He gestured to the black sphere that hung above the deck, and Alish saw Kharadron shovelling something into a furnace.

'Could we put one on the *Arbour Seed*?' she wondered aloud, and Torvald laughed.

'I see no reason why not. Now enter, all of you.'

The captain's cabin was large and well lit, a curved window in the far wall giving them a clear view past the airship's prow to the cloud-peaks beyond. Beneath it was a wooden desk scattered with charts and parchment, quills and ink, and a long-barrelled telescope.

'Welcome to my humble quarters,' Torvald said, crossing to a trolley heaped with bottles. 'Can I offer you a drink? I have ale, or... a different ale.'

Kaspar opened his mouth but Kiri shook her head. 'We're fine, thank you.'

The captain filled a tankard then took a seat, silhouetted against the window. 'Now, I brought you up here hoping to clear the air after our last conversation,' he said. 'I don't believe we fully understood each other.'

'Are you still planning to sell us into slavery?' Kiri asked. 'Because if you are, I think we understand each other just fine.'

'It's not that simple,' Torvald said, spreading his hands on the desk. 'An Ironclad costs money to keep up, and if I lost it my name would be a joke.'

'So your reputation is more important than our lives,' Kiri shot back. 'Good to know.'

Torvald hung his head, staring sadly into his glass of ale. 'I come from a family of respected cartographers,' he said, gesturing to the compass symbol on his flight suit. 'That means mapmakers, for those who don't know. For centuries this compass was a mark of quality. Our maps were highly prized in this realm and beyond, used by everyone from scholars to treasure-seekers to military commanders. We didn't just make maps of Chamon, you see, we covered every realm, even the dark ones, Ulgu and Shyish.'

Alish felt Kiri stiffen, her ears pricking up.

'We could never map the realms completely, you understand, that would take more parchment and ink than there is in existence. But what we did cover, we covered in detail – secret caves, ruined fortresses, lost cities. And we'd share that knowledge with those willing to pay for it – not anyone, of course, we wouldn't deal with Chaos types, servants of evil. But we did enough business to get very rich indeed.

'Then it all fell apart.' He frowned as dark clouds closed in around the airship. 'A decade ago I hired a new midshipman, called himself Blackhammer. At first I thought he was perfect – trustworthy, hardworking, always drumming up new business. But it was all a ruse, a way to worm himself into my good books. I left him in charge for one day and that was all it took – he scarpered, and took the maps with him. My entire livelihood, gone.

'Next I hear he's set up his own business, selling the information to anyone who'll pay. He sells cheap and he doesn't care who's buying, or what they'll use it for. And of course he's very successful, almost overnight he triples his earnings. He uses the maps for his own gain, too, planning raids and robberies. Within two years he's the most successful criminal in the region, head of an empire spanning three continents and four sky-ports. And all off the back of my maps.'

Kiri sat back. 'It's a sad story,' she admitted. 'And I'm sure that telling it makes you feel better. But it doesn't justify you selling people.'

Torvald raised his eyes. 'Don't you think I know that, girl? I just wanted you to know I don't have a choice. I'm not bad, I'm just in a very tight spot.'

Kiri snorted. 'Whatever you need to tell yourself.'

Kaspar cleared his throat subtly. 'So let me get this straight,' he said. 'If you had those maps back, you'd be rich again and you wouldn't need to sell us?'

Torvald sighed. 'I suppose so. But Blackhammer keeps the maps in the deepest treasure vault aboard his own Ironclad, the *Hammerhead*. I've sent countless men to get them back and they've all been caught, every time.'

'And those were Duardin, like you?' Kaspar asked, and Torvald nodded. 'No offence, but your race aren't exactly known for being sneaky. Someone smaller might have a chance.'

'Now, hang on,' Elio said, turning to him in dismay. 'Are you suggesting what I think you're suggesting?'

'If we got the maps back he'd let us go,' Kaspar said. 'He might even pay us.'

Torvald shrugged. 'It'd be worth a bag of aether-gold or two.'

'But we're not thieves,' Elio said. 'I mean you are, obviously, and Thanis used to be. But not the rest of us.'

Kiri turned to Torvald. 'Did you have maps of Shyish?'

The captain looked surprised. 'I had

maps of several regions in the Realm of Death. My eldest uncle made them, he was a strange one. But why in Grungni's name would you need them?'

'That's our business,' Kiri said. 'But if we steal them back for you, we get to examine them. Copy them if we need to. If you'll agree to that, I'll go along with Kaspar's plan.'

'Me too,' Thanis said, and Alish nodded.

Elio sighed. 'This is the worst idea we've had for... well, at least a day. But I suppose if everyone else wants to...'

Torvald looked at them each in turn, and again Alish could feel him judging them, trying to gauge how serious they were, and if they had a chance to pull it off. He seemed on the verge of agreeing, then he sighed and shook his head.

'It's too dangerous,' he said. 'If you were caught Blackhammer would show no mercy, and I'd feel bad for sending you in there. Besides, if it was widely known that I'd used human children to do my dirty work, I'd never live it down.'

'But we can do it,' Kaspar insisted. 'I can steal anything, from anywhere.'

Torvald smiled. 'You're bold, I'll give you that. But trust me, a Kharadron sky-city is no place for–'

He broke off as a foghorn sounded somewhere in the ship, its mournful cry echoing. He turned, squinting through the porthole at the dense clouds.

'Well, you'll see what I mean.'

Alish was aware of a darkening in the fog up ahead, something looming towards them. She covered her mouth as the fog parted and a vast shape was revealed, hanging in mid-air like the side of a cliff.

'Barak-Mhornar,' Torvald said softly. 'City of Shadow.'

The sky-port was shaped like a cylinder balanced on its end, bristling with spires and jetties like the spikes on a mace. It was crafted entirely from metal: steel plates, iron struts and ornamental statues of bronze and gold, figures of Duardin standing taller than towers. Alish couldn't help wondering how it had ever been built, what it must have cost, how many years it must have taken.

The city's base was wreathed in cloud, and a dim glow rose from the depths – some sort of energy source, she suspected. All around it she could see a swarm of airships – big Ironclads,

mid-sized frigates and tiny shapes that Alish realised were actually flying Duardin, the spheres on their backs supporting them in mid-air.

'We call those endrinriggers,' Torvald explained. 'One-man flying spheres. You should see them in battle, it's something to behold.'

They drifted over the peak of the sky-port, where tall spires jutted into the clouds. Moored to one of them was an airship ten times the size of the *Mercury Maid*, speckled with lights and rigged with massive endrins and huge, towering masts. The entire deck was silver except for a symbol painted in the centre – a black hammer.

'That's the blackguard's vessel,' Torvald growled. 'The prize for all his stealing and conniving. The *Hammerhead*, he calls it. The treasure store is under there, beneath his own cabin. What a gaudy monstrosity.'

He gestured to a golden structure rising from the silver deck, festooned with statues and lanterns and figureheads.

'It does look pretty well guarded,' Kaspar admitted, eyeing the ranks of masked and armoured Duardin who stood on the deck, huge steel weapons strapped to their backs like portable heavy artillery. 'But I've seen worse.'

'Liar,' Elio muttered. 'It looks completely impenetrable.'

'The cowardly boy is correct,' Torvald said, ignoring Elio's aggrieved stare. 'The risk is far too great.'

'Here's what I don't understand,' Alish said. 'If you're from this family of mapmakers, and that's all you've ever done, why not just make more maps? Let Blackhammer keep the ones he's got, and make better ones? It'd take a while but surely it'd be better than getting monsters to puke and selling kids into slavery?'

Torvald looked at her, and for a long moment he didn't speak. 'You ask too many questions, child,' he said at last.

'It's time for you to go back to the brig.'

Later that night Alish sat awake, listening to the rattle and din of the sky-port all around her. The *Mercury Maid* had moored to a steel jetty halfway up the vast cylinder, floating above a steel-mesh walkway. Torvald's men had emptied the Ironclad's hold, wheeling crates and barrels filled with sloshing green bile down the gangplank and piling them up on the jetty. Now all was quiet, the sky dark but for the circling torches of endrinrigger patrols and the occasional shimmer of aether-gold.

Through the jetty's floor Alish could look down into the network of walkways, ladders and loading cranes that branched from the side of the sky-port. It was like the nest of some vast steel insect, but without the sense of order and regularity that a spiderweb had. And everywhere she looked she saw Duardin – loading and unloading, bartering and haggling, gathering in rowdy groups or sitting alone, keeping watch over their possessions. She wondered if Barak-Mhornar ever slept.

Still, at least her friends could. They'd finally become too exhausted to stay awake, snoring fitfully around her while she sat gazing into the night, wondering how they kept finding themselves in these ridiculous situations. She was glad she'd seen the sky-port, and the Ironclad, and all of it. These were things she'd never forget, for as long as she lived. But she'd trade it all to be safe in her own bed at the Arbour.

A movement caught her eye and she glanced up. The jetty was silent, but for the *Mercury Maid*'s tie-ropes creaking. So what had drawn her attention? She scanned the merchandise – there. In the shadow of a three-high pile of wooden kegs, something moved. It drew back, retreating into the dark. She shielded her eyes, peering closer.

Then an airship swung overhead, docking on the jetty above. There was a lantern on the prow, shining through a circle of glass so the beam was focused and bright. The figure tried to duck but the light was too powerful, illuminating a small, desperately retreating shape. Alish saw a brown robe, a smudge of sandy hair, then it was gone.

She sat back, frowning. Could it have been one of Torvald's enemies – an agent of Blackhammer, perhaps? But she could swear it had been watching them – the five of them, not the ship itself. She was still turning it over in her head as she drifted into a restless, unhappy sleep.

CHAPTER FOUR

# Blackhammer

Alish was woken by a hand on her arm, shaking her gently.

'Get up,' Kiri said. 'Something's happening.'

The others were already awake, staring out towards the body of the sky-port. At the end of the jetty a crowd had gathered, a mob of masked, leather-clad Duardin marching towards the *Mercury Maid*. They were each waving a scrap of paper, shoving at one another in their haste to reach the Ironclad first.

A gangplank thumped down and Alish heard footsteps. Torvald Skysplitter strode into view, holding up his hands. 'What's all this?' he demanded. 'What's the fuss?'

'We want the children!' a fur-collared Duardin said, waving his paper. 'The ones you're carrying.'

Torvald glanced back towards the glass blister bolted to the bottom of the *Mercury Maid*, then he looked away quickly. *The mob can't see us,* Alish realised. *We're hidden by the shadow of the ship.*

'What children?' Torvald asked. 'I never had any beardlings, you know that.'

'These are human children,' another Duardin shouted. 'Look, it's right here.'

He handed over his parchment and Torvald frowned, tracing the words with his finger. 'Reward,' he read. 'For the delivery, unharmed, of five human children travelling on the Ironclad *Mercury Maid*. Each bears a black birthmark on the left wrist.'

Kiri gasped. 'That's impossible. Who knows we're here?'

'We're in a whole different realm, for Sigmar's sake,' Elio agreed.

Kaspar said nothing, just staring out as the gaggle of Duardin pushed closer.

'Where are you hiding them?' one cried.

'Hand them over!' yelled another.

Torvald looked back towards the blister, then down at the paper in his hand. He pursed his lips, then nodded to one of his henchmen. 'Fetch them out.'

The older Duardin strode beneath the airship, taking a set of keys from his belt. He reached up, fumbling with the side of the blister, and suddenly Alish realised what was about to happen.

'Wait,' she said. 'Just–'

The floor dropped away and out they tumbled, landing hard on the jetty. The crowd spotted them and pushed closer, as Torvald raised both hands. 'Now, I will start the bidding at five thousand–'

'STOP!'

The voice was so loud that Alish felt

the steel grate tremble. She picked herself up as a figure muscled through the crowd, shoving the others aside. He was tall for a Duardin and broad too, his belly bulging like a beer barrel. His bald head was riddled with scars and his mask was encrusted with precious stones – diamonds for the teeth, rubies around the eyes. He swung a massive mallet made of obsidian, its head notched in a hundred places.

'Blackhammer,' Thanis hissed beneath her breath.

His black-masked cronies moved in, holding the other Duardin back while their boss drew out his own piece of paper, holding it up. He pointed at the children with one massive finger.

'Those are my property,' he said. 'And I'm taking them.'

The crowd backed away dutifully but Torvald stepped forward, coming between Blackhammer and the children. 'Arkanaut admiral,' he said. 'What a pleasant surprise.'

'Stow it, Skysplitter,' Blackhammer scowled. 'And get out of my way, I'm taking those brats.'

Torvald nodded. 'How much are you prepared to offer? I was about to begin bidding at ten thousand, you're welcome to take part.'

Blackhammer sneered. 'I'll give you five hundred, which is twice what you'd have been expecting in the slave market. Remember, I'm the power on this sky-port. You want to trade, you trade with me.'

Torvald drew himself up, and for a moment Alish thought he was going to stand his ground. The men from the *Mercury Maid* watched cautiously. Blackhammer glanced at his own black-clad bodyguards, who stood ready.

Then Torvald sighed and shook his head. 'Take them.'

Kiri reacted first, throwing herself at the old Duardin, taking him by surprise and knocking him off his feet. 'Come on,' she told the others. 'Run!'

They ducked beneath the *Mercury Maid*'s floating hull, sprinting back along the jetty. Thanis grabbed a hooked pole as they ran, swinging it down and around as a gang of Torvald's men ran to cut them off. Two tripped over the pole and went flying, the others leapt clear and kept coming.

They reached the stacks of crates, and Elio and Kaspar shoved them over, blocking their pursuers. Alish could see Blackhammer's henchmen moving in, the combined force of silver and black-masked Duardin racing towards them. She grabbed a keg and pushed as hard as she could, toppling it. Green bile flooded out, splashing across the jetty. The metal began to hiss and the Duardin skidded wildly, three of them losing their footing and tumbling over one another, their padded suits covered in stinking slime.

Then a musket shot rang out, the bullet thudding into a crate near Alish's head. Kiri pulled her down, and behind them they heard Torvald's furious bellow.

'Don't shoot the merchandise! The paper says unharmed!'

Alish scrabbled around a last stack of boxes and onto the open jetty. She looked back, seeing the furious Duardin scrambling over the toppled crates. Then to her amazement she saw something else – a tiny figure cowering behind a keg, trying desperately not to be noticed. She stepped forward, reaching down and grabbing hold of a white, quivering arm.

'You!' she said.

The ragged boy looked up at her, trembling. Scratch looked even paler than when they'd last seen him, down in the Skaven warren. His ratlike clothes were gone and the makeshift whiskers had been wiped from his face. Instead he wore a tatty brown jacket and a belt; he even had shoes on his feet.

'What is he doing here?' Elio asked. 'How is this even possible?'

'I don't know,' Kiri said. 'But we don't

have time for it. Thanis, bring him.'

Thanis rolled her eyes and tugged but the boy held back, shaking his head. Then there was a shout close by as the Duardin closed in, kicking past the last stack of boxes. Scratch took one look at them and stumbled into Thanis's arms.

'Go!' she shouted and the others backed away, racing along the jetty.

But now they were running out of room – up ahead the walkway ended, narrowing to a point. Kaspar turned aside, picking up speed as he ran to the edge. Alish's heart raced as she saw him leap out into empty space, arms waving as he plummeted downwards, landing on another jetty a short distance below.

'Elio, you next!' Kiri shouted. He gave a howl as he jumped, his legs kicking madly as he soared through the air, landing hard and rolling. Thanis clutched Scratch and followed, then Alish gritted her teeth and forced herself over the edge, the jetty rushing up to meet her.

She landed, shaken but unhurt as Kiri dropped beside her. Their pursuers stood on the jetty above, yelling and gesturing but unwilling to make the leap.

'This way,' Kaspar said, leading them back towards the sky-port. 'If we can get inside we might be able to lose them.'

The steel face of Barak-Mhornar loomed up, dotted with dark openings like caves in the side of a precipice. The jetty led towards the grandest of these, an arched entranceway with bronze figures carved around the rim. They picked up speed, darting beneath gangplanks and bounding over coiled ropes, ignoring the shouts from behind them and the startled faces of passing Duardin.

The sounds around them changed as they entered the sky-port, voices echoing as the walls closed in. The tunnel was high and broad, its curved plate walls gleaming with moisture. Duardin bustled by, leading pack animals, hefting sacks and boxes or pushing carts heaped with crates. There were so many of them, Alish thought, as many as there were people in Lifestone, or even more. This truly was a city in the sky.

Then Elio cried, 'Look!' and she turned. Another walkway led down from above, a steep ramp joined to the higher jetty. Down it stormed Blackhammer, his men fanning out around him, shoving any passing Duardin out of their way.

'It's no use,' Kaspar said. 'We can't outrun them. And they'll follow us wherever we try to hide.'

'Not necessarily,' Thanis said, holding Scratch with one hand and pointing with the other. On the far side of the tunnel a hatch was set into the wall – small and narrow and lined with steel. As they watched a Duardin strode up to it, dragging a wicker basket. He held the hatch open, tipping the basket so that the contents tumbled out – Alish saw turnip-tops and rotten fruit, scraps of cloth and animal bones.

'Come on,' Kiri said, running over. 'It might be our only chance.'

She held the hatch open and Elio scrambled in first, looking down uncertainly.

'Are you sure about this? It could be an awful long way d– aaaaaagh!'

Kiri had given him a hard shove and he vanished into the dark; Alish heard his cry trail off, then silence.

'Him next,' Kiri said, pointing at Scratch. 'Then you, Kaspar. Make sure he doesn't get away.'

Kaspar nodded, climbing after the ragged boy. He shot them a last, uncertain smile then pushed off, sliding down into the dark.

'You should go next,' Alish told Kiri, but the girl shook her head.

'I don't think so,' she said. 'Come on, climb up.'

Alish scrambled into the hatch, clinging to the frame. Then over Thanis's shoulder she saw a commotion breaking out, Duardin shoving closer. A figure appeared, taller than the rest, striding towards them. Blackhammer.

'Wait,' Alish said, grabbing Kiri's arm. 'You'll never make it, there's no time.'

Kiri tipped her head on one side. 'I know,' she said, and gave Alish a shove. The last thing she heard was a yell of defiance as she rocketed away into the chute.

## CHAPTER FIVE

# The Conveyor

Alish picked up speed as she slid down the liquid-slick rubbish chute, veering left and right as it descended through the sky-port. Other shafts joined theirs, other openings leading back up into the vast structure. But she was moving too quickly, unable to slow down or grab on.

She could hear the others below her, clattering and thumping as the tunnel widened. But she could hear nothing behind her, no movement, no voices. She knew what this meant. Thanis and Kiri had been captured.

Suddenly the tunnel angled almost

vertically, and her heart hammered as she tumbled, scraping against the sides. What if there was no bottom, what if the Kharadron simply tipped their rubbish out into the clouds? This might have been the worst mistake they'd ever made.

Then she heard a shout and saw the ground rising up, a muddle of black and silver rushing to meet her. She saw Kaspar's startled face, one hand raised, but it was too late. She landed right on top of him, slamming him down into a bed of damp, smelly refuse. He let out a breathless 'oof' and she rolled over.

'Nice soft landing?' Kaspar asked resentfully, struggling to his feet.

Alish blushed. 'It's not like I had a choice.'

They were in a large circular tunnel with a slight downward slope, the riveted steel walls dripping with condensation. Above them pale light leaked from a series of openings – the mouths of the various chutes, she realised, as a tangle of refuse came tumbling out of one, machine parts crashing down some distance away. In fact, the majority of the rubbish appeared to be metallic – airship components and bits of broken walkway, rusted hatches and bent sky-hooks. The rest must have been food waste, because the smell was appalling.

'Where's Thanis?' Elio asked. 'And Kiri?'

Alish frowned. 'Blackhammer's men were right on top of them.'

Kaspar sighed. 'Great. The only ones who knew what they were doing.'

'Hey,' Elio said. 'I'm a leader too. I got us out of the Skaven warren, remember?'

'Most of us,' Kaspar reminded him, nodding at Scratch. The boy crouched on his haunches, not speaking; Alish wasn't even sure if he could. But she felt like he understood every word they said.

'Why did you run away?' Elio asked

him. ‘That night in the warren, why did you run when we were trying to help you?’

Scratch looked up at him nervously, holding both hands at his waist as though guarding something. Elio reached down and snatched at the boy’s belt, tugging something loose.

‘What’s this?’ he asked as Scratch swiped at it, whining. It was a small leather pouch containing several sheets of paper, printed on one side. ‘Reward for the capture of… Hey, this is the same notice those Duardin had!’

‘That was you?’ Alish asked Scratch. ‘You put these around the sky-port?’

The ragged boy bowed his head guiltily, then he nodded.

‘They must be from Kreech,’ Elio said. ‘Look, his spelling’s awful.’

‘He must have sent Scratch to find us,’ Alish said.

‘But why didn’t he come himself?’ Kaspar asked.

Scratch frowned, making claws with his

hands and fangs with his teeth, then mimicking someone swinging an axe.

'Of course,' Elio said. 'If the Kharadron found a Skaven in their sky-city they'd kill it, no questions asked. So he sent his little lackey instead.'

'How did Kreech know we were here?' Alish asked, but Scratch just shrugged.

Kaspar peered up, squinting into the dark. 'There has to be a way out of here.'

Suddenly the floor shook and he looked around in surprise. The trembling came again, the junk pile shuddering.

'What's happening?' Alish asked. 'Why is–'

There was a crash and a slam, and red light flooded the tunnel. Down the slope a hatch had opened, and through it she could see flames rising. Cogs whirred and the floor started to move, sliding slowly down towards the open hatch.

'We're on a belt,' she realised as junk toppled all around them. They were being drawn slowly but steadily towards the flames, the sides of the tunnel inching past.

Then in the open hatchway something else moved, a part of the ceiling detaching and slamming down, crushing the refuse as it slid by. There were spikes on it like teeth, impaling the larger pieces of rubbish and grinding them to pieces. It rose once more, cogs clicking, then smacked back down.

'Everybody, move!' Elio shouted, grabbing Scratch by the collar.

They scrambled over a pile of junk, clawing up the heap of metal and down the other side. They landed on the surface of the belt itself; it was soft and springy, probably leather, Alish decided. Then she saw a wave of rubbish rising over them – something had snagged on the side of the tunnel and was holding the refuse back, causing it to pile higher and higher.

'We've got to climb,' Kaspar said. 'Quick, before it falls!'

He threw himself at the rising heap, holding out a hand for Scratch to grab onto. The boy climbed, Elio shoving him from beneath. Alish felt the heat on her back, saw the light grow around them as they drew closer to that terrible furnace.

She was halfway up the rubbish pile when the wave broke, sending metal and rotting food raining down around her. She could feel her feet slipping as the junk slid away, crashing down beneath her.

Then a hand shot out and grabbed her wrist, pulling her in. Elio stood on the back of a dented steel door, his arm straining as he hauled her up. There was a crash behind them as that huge jaw slammed down, flattening everything beneath it.

Then with a clunk the hatch closed and darkness fell once more.

Alish sank down, loosening her collar and gasping for air. 'That was… too close.'

'We need to get back up the tunnel,' Kaspar said. 'In case it happens again.'

Elio nodded, helping Alish up. They scaled the rubbish until they reached what they hoped was a safe distance, resting on the back of a huge Ironclad hull-plate. More junk kept dropping all around them – scrap and bones and stinking liquid.

'All we've done is buy time,' Kaspar said. 'That masher will start up again.'

'So what are we supposed to do?' Elio said, gazing up at the openings overhead. 'Even if we could reach one of those, we couldn't climb all the way back up.'

'Maybe there's something down here we can use,' Alish mused.

There was a sudden crash as a large object landed in the tunnel not far away – a black shape tipping towards them. Alish looked at it, and couldn't believe her eyes.

'Is that... It can't...'

'It's the *Arbour Seed*!' Elio cried.

They waded towards it through the rubbish. The airship lay toppled, its balloon a tattered rag. But the gondola was still intact, and so were most of the steam-pipes.

'I guess Torvald had no use for her,' Alish said, inspecting the battered gauges. 'So he just threw her away.'

'Or perhaps he did it on purpose,' Kaspar said. 'Look, what's this?'

He reached under the portside bench,

pulling out a cloth sack. He upended it, sending the contents spilling onto the deck. To her amazement Alish saw her hammer and tools, Kiri's catapult and Vertigan's staff. A piece of paper fluttered out last, and Elio grabbed it.

'Your friends are on the *Hammerhead*,' he read. 'So are my maps. Look for this symbol, the compass.'

Kaspar laughed, clapping his hands together. 'So he wants to take us up on our offer. I knew he'd see sense.'

Elio gulped. 'I guess we don't have

a choice, if we want to get Kiri and Thanis.'

'But how do we get to the *Hammerhead*?' Alish wondered. 'The *Arbour Seed*'s a wreck, it can't fly. Torvald knows that.'

'Is there a way to patch it up?' Kaspar asked. 'Any way to sew the balloon back together?'

Alish shook her head. 'It took days to make the first time. By then we'll be toast.'

'Great,' Elio said, kicking Torvald's sack. 'Fat lot of use he turned out to... Hey, what's this?'

He reached into the sack, pulling out something that had snagged in the bottom – a tiny wooden casket the size of his palm. He prised it open and golden light poured out, illuminating his surprised face.

'Aether-gold!' he whispered. 'That's our way out!'

'Not so fast,' Alish said. 'You don't just need the ship and the gold, what we really need is a... is a...' She tailed off, looking around. 'Everyone, spread out. We're looking for a metal sphere about as tall as a person. If we can find one, and if I can fix it to this bucket of bolts, we might have a chance before–'

There was a crunch from the far end of the tunnel, the sound of cogs whirring into life.

'Before we get flattened and fried,' Kaspar finished for her, as firelight flooded over them.

CHAPTER SIX

# The Seed Reborn

It was Scratch who found the endrin sphere, jumping up and down and waving his arms frantically as the masher crunched and the furnace roared. Elio and Kaspar struggled towards him and between them they managed to roll the sphere back to where Alish was waiting in the *Arbour Seed*. They were sweating in the furnace heat, and the masher stamped noisily as the conveyor belt groaned beneath them.

Alish inspected the sphere. 'It's a bit dented, but it'll do. Now, I bet this is the inflow pipe, and this must be the regulator. So if I just fix this on here...'

She grabbed a hose from the *Arbour Seed*, jamming it on. Then she twisted a gauge and heard a loud kettle-like hiss, a gurgling coming from deep inside the endrin sphere.

'Whatever you're doing,' Kaspar said, 'you need to do it faster.'

Alish looked over her shoulder. They were drawing close to the masher, the airship sliding towards that terrible crushing jaw. There wouldn't be enough time.

'We need to slow ourselves down,' she told them. 'Remember before, that wave that rose up? We need that to happen again.'

Kaspar nodded, jumping out of the airship with Elio on his heels. Alish turned back to the endrin sphere, and tried to roll it over so she could access some of the sockets on the far side. The thing was heavy; she struggled to lift it, groaning in frustration as it weighed down on top of her.

Then she felt hands shoving at the sphere, turning it. Scratch grinned, and together they managed to roll it over. 'We need to fix that strut onto there,' Alish said, and Scratch nodded, gathering up a pair of loose bolts and hurrying to the back of the airship. He crouched, locking the strut to the endrin sphere. She nodded, impressed.

Then there was a screech and a groan and she looked up. Elio and Kaspar had found a long steel pole and jammed it into the side of the tunnel. Sparks were flying as it scraped and tore. They thrust the other end into the pile of refuse, creating a barrier that the junk started to pile up against. Then they scrambled back to the *Arbour Seed* as the refuse heaped around them, their faces grimy and fearful in the flickering light.

'Almost there,' Alish said, plugging in the regulator pipe and stepping back, wiping her brow. The air was stifling, the furnace raging like an angry animal. The *Arbour Seed* started to tip, borne up on the surge of junk. She looked at the dented black sphere attached to the old balloon struts and couldn't believe that it would really work, that this pile of scrap metal and splintered wood could actually fly them out of here.

She took out the box Torvald had given them, opening the lid.

'Here goes nothing.'

The aether-gold sparkled as she shook it into the pipe, funnelling it with her

hands. Then she fastened the loose end to one of her old pressure gauges, twisting the dial slowly, cautiously.

Nothing happened.

There was a snap and a groan and she saw the long pipe bend in two, the wave of junk crashing down behind them. The furnace was close now; she could feel its heat on her face, feel the floor shake as the masher slammed down.

'Should we abandon ship?' Kaspar yelled. 'Is it going to fly or not?'

'I don't know!' Alish shrieked. 'I've done everything I can think of!'

Then she looked down, her mouth dropping open. 'I'm so stupid,' she said. 'Wrong pipe!' She tugged out both pipes, fitting the outflow to the regulator and the inflow to the pressure gauge. The *Arbour Seed* began to shake, the endrin sphere humming like a swarm of dagger-wasps.

Then they jerked into the air, the struts and guy ropes going taut. The masher slammed down, missing the stern by a hair's breadth – the next one would flatten them. She saw Elio and Scratch silhouetted in the firelight, their eyes wide with terror.

'Hang on to something,' she said, and opened the regulator.

The *Arbour Seed* shot forward like a rocket, skidding against the sides of the tunnel, scraping the tops of the junk pile below. Alish clung on desperately, one hand on the wheel, the other gripping the regulator lever. She pulled it back, trying to slow them down, but it didn't have much of an effect. So she reached for the altitude gauge, twisting it so that the airship began to tilt, aiming nose first towards the ceiling.

There was only one opening large enough for them to fit through – the same one through which the *Arbour Seed* had dropped. She aimed for it, hoping it was open at the top.

They shot upwards like a ball through a cannon, the struts groaning as the endrin sphere rattled and roared. Elio held on to Scratch as Kaspar crashed into the stern.

'Sorry!' Alish shouted. 'But this is the only way.'

The walls of the chute narrowed, and the hull of the airship bumped and scraped against them. But she could see light up ahead, a patch of gold against the grey walls of the tunnel.

They exploded from the opening, startling a pair of Duardin who were trying to dump an entire rhinox carcass. Alish shuddered, imagining what would've happened if it had come down while they were coming up. One of the Duardin shook his fist as they spiralled away, twisting into the tunnel and picking up speed.

Alish gripped the wheel, trying in vain to control the ship as it bucked and rolled. They were moving through what looked like the sky-port's living quarters; she saw cook-pots smoking and hammocks strung from the walls, Duardin waking with a cry as the airship rocketed overhead. They slammed through a succession of washing lines strung across the tunnel, sending jackets and trousers flying in every direction. Scratch let out a muffled cry, tearing something large and woolly away from his face – it looked like a pair of Duardin undergarments. Still, at least they were clean.

Then the tunnel came to an abrupt end, a wider hallway crossing it. Alish gritted her teeth and spun the wheel,

slamming them sideways into the next passage, scraping the corner as they screamed through. Suddenly the walls and the ceiling opened out and they were in a huge domed space, echoing with shouts and chatter.

It was a market, she saw, the huge circular floor covered with stalls and awnings. Duardin strode through, bartering and haggling, the din of their voices filling the vast space. Smoke rose from a blacksmith's stall and she heard the clang of hammers. Everything she could imagine seemed to be for sale down there – weapons and armour, meat and mead, clothes and boots and row upon row of airship parts: sky-hooks, hull plates and shiny endrin spheres, floating from tethers of rope. *Give me a bag of gold,* she thought, *and an afternoon in here, and I could build ten ships better than this one.*

'Go left!' Elio shouted. 'I see a way out!'

On the far side of the market was

a tunnel larger than the rest, a huge archway rising above the steel floor. And through it she could see daylight, shafts of gold slanting into the chamber. She turned the wheel and they curved smoothly, dipping low as they entered the tunnel. Duardin looked up, pointing and jeering, but by then they were already gone, speeding through the clamouring space and out into the open.

'Hey, you're getting good at this,' Kaspar said as they dipped beneath a jetty, avoiding a tangle of cables and rising swiftly on the far side.

Alish smiled. 'You just have to think fast,' she said, ducking as the endrin sphere crashed through a rope-and-plank walkway, tearing it to shreds. 'Um, faster than that.'

The sun's last light broke through the clouds – the day was dimming rapidly.

'We need to go up,' Kaspar said. 'The *Hammerhead* was moored at the top of the sky-port, remember?'

'Do we want to go there right

away?' Alish asked. 'Shouldn't we land somewhere and make a plan?'

'The longer we leave it, the more chance there is of us being spotted. Blackhammer's got eyes all over this city, and I bet they're all looking for us.'

Alish sighed. 'I guess you're right. Well, there she is.'

She pointed past the prow of the *Arbour Seed*, out into the thickening clouds. The huge black Ironclad jutted from the fog, lanterns beaming on the deck. It resembled a steel blade in a blacksmith's forge, gleaming with its own light, drenched in steam and smoke above the smouldering lights of the sky-port. It was moored to a huge pontoon with ropes thicker than Alish's torso, and squinting she could see masked sentries on the deck, standing in serried ranks by the railing.

'Take us up and over,' Kaspar whispered. 'Stay as close to the clouds as you can.'

Alish skirted the fringes of the fog – the *Arbour Seed* was unlit, so from the *Hammerhead*'s deck they'd be a black dot against blacker clouds. But if any of those sentries had a spyglass and happened to look up just at the wrong moment…

'There's Blackhammer's quarters,' Kaspar said, pointing to the large gold structure rising from the deck. 'And look, that's our way down.'

From the roof of the cabin a single mast rose, topped with a circular crow's nest. In it Alish could see a Duardin keeping watch, smoking a pipe as he rested his back against the railing.

'Take us closer,' Kaspar whispered. 'Pass me your hammer. And throw me that rope. I've got an idea.'

## CHAPTER SEVEN

# The Hammerhead

They lashed a loose rope to the railing and Kaspar took hold, descending hand over hand into the fog. Alish kept the *Arbour Seed* steady as denser clouds rolled in, hiding the crow's nest from view. There was a cry, brief and swiftly silenced. When the fog parted she saw the Duardin lying prone as Kaspar beckoned them down. Alish took hold of the tiller, bringing them in and preparing to dock.

'Don't worry,' Kaspar assured her. 'He'll just wake up with a rotten headache.'

Alish retrieved her hammer, stashing

it in the airship – she couldn't climb that mast with a weight on her back. Then she stepped out, beckoning to Scratch.

'You really want to bring him?' Elio asked. 'What if he tries something?'

Scratch looked up with wide, innocent eyes, and Alish took pity. 'Come on, he's one of us now. Aren't you?'

The boy nodded, and nuzzled against her side like a wolf-pup.

They clambered silently down the mast, following a ladder of struts hammered into the steel. They reached the roof of the golden cabin and Kaspar crouched, shuffling to the edge and peering over. He beckoned, and dropped onto a shallow balcony. Just as on the *Mercury Maid*, a large circular porthole faced towards the prow of the ship. Kaspar inspected it, looking for a latch. He pushed the top and the porthole flipped over, the bottom end catching his ankles, tipping him up and into the room beyond.

He bit back a cry of surprise, sliding on the tilting glass and lowering himself down. Then he held it open so the others could duck under.

'No guards,' Alish whispered. 'That's lucky.'

'Perhaps he doesn't think anyone would dare break in,' Elio said.

'Or maybe he doesn't trust any of his people enough to leave them alone in his private chamber,' Kaspar suggested.

The cabin was large and gaudy, every piece of furniture trimmed with gold.

Red velvet curtains hung from the walls, patterned with Duardin runes in golden thread, and the pelt of some shaggy white beast lay stretched out on the mahogany floor.

'Where now?' Alish whispered, and Kaspar nodded to a large door on the far side.

'Let's see where that leads.'

They crept towards it but suddenly Elio paused, pointing down. A corner of the rug had been folded back, one of the beast's spiked paws caught in its fur. Beneath it Alish could see a wink of metal.

'A hinge,' she whispered.

'Torvald said that Blackhammer's treasure room was beneath his private chambers,' Elio remembered. 'Maybe this hatch leads–'

'Right this way,' a voice boomed suddenly. 'After you, old friend.'

They threw themselves across the room, ducking behind the curtains as the far door swung open. Elio pulled

Scratch down as two Duardin strode through.

'We're not friends, Blackhammer,' one said, and Alish recognised Torvald's gruff tones. 'You stole from me, let's not pretend otherwise. And now you've done it again. If you don't pay for the merchandise you took, I'll take it back.'

'But I didn't get all of it, did I?' Blackhammer retorted. 'The reward was for five children, and three will be crushed to cinders by now.'

'So what about the two you have?' Torvald asked. 'Where are you keeping them?'

Blackhammer strode to a large black barrel that hung on the wall, filling a flagon with ale. He didn't offer one to Torvald. 'That's none of your lookout,' he said. 'But they're staying with me. Those two have caused enough trouble.'

Kaspar gestured towards the open door and Alish nodded. They hugged the wall, staying behind the heavy, hanging curtains. Then they darted around the door while both Duardin had their backs turned. Elio followed, one hand on Scratch's arm.

They emerged into a dimly lit corridor, one end of which opened onto the airship's deck while the other led to a set of steps leading deeper into the belly of the Ironclad.

'I bet Thanis and Kiri are close by,' Kaspar whispered as they crept towards the stairs. 'Like his treasure, they're worth something. He'd want to keep an–'

'You ungrateful wretches!' a voice cried suddenly from the bottom of the steps. A door slammed open, a white-coated Duardin stumbling backwards through it. He held a tray in one hand and his clothes and face were covered with brown liquid and chunks of cooked meat. 'I make you a perfectly good stew and you chuck it all over me! Well, it's the last you'll get. You can stay in there and starve, the pair of you!'

Alish looked at Elio. His face broke into a smile.

The cook stormed away and they hurried down the steps, pushing through the door. The *Hammerhead*'s brig was lined with cells, but only the last one was occupied. A pair of figures sat hunched against the wall, their heads on their knees.

'Didn't we tell you to get lost?' Kiri snarled as the door hinges creaked.

'Sure, if that's what you want,' Kaspar replied. 'We can always rescue you later.'

The two girls jumped up, grabbing the bars.

'You're alive!' Thanis said. 'I mean, we knew you would be.'

'No we didn't,' Kiri admitted. 'But we hoped.'

Kaspar pulled out his leather wallet, opening it to reveal a row of slender lock-picks. He crouched by the cell door, getting to work.

'We fixed the *Arbour Seed*,' Alish said. 'It's faster than ever now.'

'And we found out who sent those

notes,' Elio added, telling them about Scratch and Kreech and the reward for their capture. 'What we don't know is how in Sigmar's name he found out we were here.'

Kiri frowned. 'Our first priority is to get as far away from here as we can,' she said. 'Everyone on the sky-port's after us, and there's only one person we know who might lift a finger to help us.'

'Torvald,' Alish nodded. 'But only if we steal his maps.'

'We think the treasure vault's underneath us,' Elio said. 'We saw a kind of hatch in Blackhammer's private rooms.'

'So did we,' Thanis nodded. 'He took us in there to lecture us about how rich and powerful he is. It was torture.'

'But he's in there now,' Alish pointed out. 'We can't get past him.'

'There might be another way,' Kiri said, pointing to the back of the room where a ventilation panel was bolted to the wall – too small for a Duardin to climb through, but maybe just wide enough for the five of them.

Alish took out her screw-loosener and the bolts on the panel came away easily. Scratch bounded over to help and she smiled gratefully. 'I'm okay, I've got it.'

Then a voice roared outside and her head whipped round.

'I'm telling you not to go in there!' Blackhammer bellowed, his boots clanging down the steps. 'Those children are my property.'

'Don't you give me orders,' Torvald replied. 'I'm taking them, and that's final.'

'Kaspar, how long?' Kiri hissed.

'Quicker if you don't talk to me,' he shot back, peering into the lock.

'I'll have your ship for this, Skysplitter,' Blackhammer growled, and then three things happened at once.

The door to the brig slammed open and Torvald backed into the room, his sturdy frame filling the doorway. The last bolt dropped into Alish's hand and the ventilation hatch dropped away, revealing a black opening behind. And the door to the cell swung wide, Kaspar jumping to his feet.

Hearing the creak of hinges, Torvald turned briefly and his eyes went wide. He saw Kiri and Thanis stepping out of the cell, and Elio wriggling into the ventilation shaft. Then he turned back, spreading his shoulders to block the doorway.

'Actually, I've changed my mind,' he said, gesturing fiercely behind his back. 'I don't need to see them. You were right, they're your property.'

Blackhammer gave a grunt of surprise, as Alish shoved Scratch into the shaft and climbed in, Thanis on her heels.

'What do you mean, changed your mind?' the big Duardin asked suspiciously. 'What are you trying to pull?'

'You made a good point, that's all,'

Torvald said. 'I don't want to risk my ship. Really, I don't know what I was thinking.'

The light in the shaft dimmed as Kiri replaced the panel, tugging it as tight as she could. 'Elio,' she whispered as they squirmed deeper into the darkness. 'What can you see?'

'Not much,' his voice came back. 'There's a bit that goes along, and a bit that goes down.'

'We should go down,' Kaspar hissed. 'The treasure vault should be sort of under us and over there. That way.'

'Stop prodding me,' Elio protested. 'I've really just had enough of sliding along narrow passages for one day, all right? Just for once I'd like to–'

There was a crash behind them and Kiri yelled out. Alish looked back to see a hand reaching into the shaft, grabbing her ankle.

'I knew it!' Blackhammer roared. 'You little thieves, stop right– aaagh!'

Kiri had kicked as hard as she could,

mashing his knuckles with the sole of her boot. He let go and she scrambled forward, shoving Thanis ahead of her. The big girl piled into Alish, who nudged Scratch, whose head slammed into Kaspar's back. Elio gave a cry, and Alish heard a scraping sound as he tumbled into the dark.

Blackhammer's face disappeared and they heard heavy footsteps in the brig, followed by the slam of a door.

'Where's Elio?' Alish asked fearfully. 'Is he okay?'

'Elio,' Kaspar called out. 'Where are you?'

They heard a distant, echoing groan. 'I fell,' his voice came back. 'But I'm okay. Wait, I'll just...' They heard him moving around. 'Now jump down, all of you. One at a time.'

Alish heard Kaspar shuffling forward; he dropped and she heard a faint gasp of surprise.

'This is madness,' Thanis said as Scratch dropped after him. 'Jumping around in the dark. I hope Elio knows what he's doing.'

'Of course he does,' Kiri said, but she didn't sound entirely certain.

Alish pushed herself over, sliding down a gentle incline that steepened suddenly. She fell through an opening, plummeting through the air.

Then she landed abruptly, dropping onto something soft and brightly coloured. Kaspar reached for her, pulling her in. She'd landed on a huge tapestry patterned with Duardin warriors and Kharadron airships, all outlined in golden thread. And looking up she saw other objects in the gloom – plates and goblets, statues and figurines, swords and breastplates.

'We found it,' she breathed. 'Blackhammer's treasure room.'

Then she heard shouts and stamping feet, and somewhere a bell began to ring.

'They're coming after us,' Kiri said, picking herself up. 'Let's find these maps.'

CHAPTER EIGHT

# The Vault

The treasure vault was vast, lantern light leaking through high barred windows from the deck above. Everywhere she looked Alish saw riches – sacks of doubloons, strings of jewelled necklaces, golden goblets overflowing with gemstones and paintings of stern-looking Duardin glowering from ornate frames. There didn't seem to be any order to it – everything was just heaped together, piled almost to the ceiling.

'Well, look at this place,' Thanis said, peering around in wonder. 'Pity we didn't find it when we were living rough on the streets, right, Kaspar?'

'Everyone, stop gawping and search,' Kiri said as shouts echoed through the Ironclad. 'We must be looking for a box or a case or something, anything that could hold a lot of maps.'

'That doesn't narrow it down,' Elio said. 'Look, there's a golden chest over there, and a big wooden one over there.'

'So go and check if there are any maps inside,' Kiri said impatiently.

Alish picked her way through,

accidentally stepping on a porcelain wyvern, breaking off one of its wings. She came across a steel casket filled with silver musket balls and another heaped with ladies' clothes, all crushed velvet and lace.

'What would Blackhammer need these for?' she wondered aloud. 'I don't think they'd suit him.'

'There's a door over here,' Kaspar called out. 'Must be the delivery entrance. It's locked, but I'll try to get it open while the rest of you keep hunting for the maps.'

'Hang on,' Alish said suddenly, holding up a hand. 'I've got an idea. Torvald's note said the maps were on the *Hammerhead*, then he followed it with his symbol, the compass. We should be looking for that.'

'Clever girl,' a voice said, and they looked up. A hatch had opened overhead and Blackhammer peered down, his face as red as the velvet curtains Alish could see behind him.

He reached through, a flintlock pistol grasped in his hand. He squinted down the barrel, aiming into the dark. Kiri grabbed Alish, pulling her aside as the bullet struck a large silver-framed mirror, shattering it.

'That was a warning shot,' Blackhammer shouted. 'You're worth money, so I don't want to hurt you. But if you try to steal anything that belongs to me, all bets will be off.'

They heard him reloading the pistol, and Kiri cursed. 'Next time he won't miss.'

'But look,' Alish said, pointing at the mirror. Through the shattered glass she could see a large wooden crate, and emblazoned on it was Torvald's mark, the sign of the compass. Someone had tried to scratch it off with blunt strokes, but the symbol was unmistakable.

They shoved the mirror aside and Alish tried to lift the lid, but it was chained and sealed with a padlock. It raised just high enough for her to peer inside, and in the dim light she saw a collection of scrolls, all sealed with wax.

Then another shot rang out and they ducked. The bullet buried itself in the wall.

'Thanis, take an end,' Kiri said, and they lifted the crate, struggling towards the door where Kaspar knelt. Blackhammer spotted them and gave a shout of frustration. Alish looked back to see him climbing through the hatch, his broad frame barely squeezing through the gap.

'You and you, cut them off,' he shouted, gesturing to someone in the cabin above. Then he began to climb down, the rope creaking beneath him.

'Got it,' Kaspar said and the door swung open, revealing a long metal ramp leading up into the light. Kaspar, Elio and Scratch started up the ramp, followed closely by Kiri and Thanis, hefting the chest. As Alish tugged the door shut behind her she saw

Blackhammer dropping, landing hard. Then she put her head down and ran after the others.

At the top of the ramp was a steel grille and Kaspar shoved it open, stepping up onto the broad, flat deck. Alish joined him just as a pair of Blackhammer's guards rounded the corner of the cabin and spotted them, pointing.

'This way,' Kaspar shouted, running to the foot of a ladder that led to the roof of Blackhammer's quarters. Alish squinted at the crow's nest above. It seemed an awfully long way off. She started to climb after Kaspar, Elio not far behind.

Then the guards were on them, grabbing at Scratch as he raced up the ladder after Elio. Kiri and Thanis looked at each other and nodded, then swung the chest between them, letting it slide across the deck into the two guards. The Duardin were thrown off their feet, skidding helplessly. The chest bumped against the wall of the cabin and Kiri and Thanis retrieved it, then started struggling up the ladder after the rest of the group.

Alish followed Kaspar towards the crow's nest. The two Duardin had recovered themselves and were climbing after them, fury on their faces. Back on the deck she could see Blackhammer emerging from the hatch, shouting encouragement to his men as they scaled the mast with surprising speed.

Thanis and Kiri had to fight for every rung, Thanis hoisting the chest by a handle on the side while Kiri shoved it from below. But the Duardin were closing on them, knives clutched between their teeth.

Suddenly Alish remembered, reaching into her pocket. 'Kiri!' she shouted. 'Catch!'

She tossed down the catapult and Kiri caught it one-handed, Thanis taking the weight while Kiri plucked a piece of shot from the pouch at her waist.

She took careful aim and let loose: the nearest Duardin yowled as the shot struck his knuckles with a crack. He lost his grip on the mast and slid down, knocking his companion flying. The pair of them landed flat on the cabin's roof, as Blackhammer cursed and bellowed on the deck.

They reached the crow's nest, and Elio and Scratch helped the two girls to haul the chest over the railing. Alish leapt into the *Arbour Seed* and started up the endrin, hearing it thrum. Below them, a group of Blackhammer's men had gathered on the deck, strapping heavy packs on their backs with black endrin spheres attached. She saw Blackhammer himself among them, clipping into a rig of his own. He thrust a pair of pistols into his belt, looking furiously up towards the crow's nest.

'Everyone, hang on tight,' Alish said as Thanis heaved the chest over the side, dropping it into the gondola.

'We've got company.'

The *Arbour Seed* rose into the clouds, wobbling slightly with the increased weight. Then Alish opened the regulator and they slammed forward, cutting a trail through the fog. Glancing back she saw the endrinriggers rising in formation from the *Hammerhead*'s deck, pairs of them turning to follow the little airship. Blackhammer brought up the rear, barking orders as his cohorts took to the sky.

The foremost riggers fired their pistols, and bullets glanced off the steel endrin. For a moment Alish was confused – why were they firing at the sphere? Then she realised – they were trying to disable the airship without damaging the merchandise inside.

She grabbed the wheel, angling back towards the sky-port. If those riggers caught them in the open there'd be no escape – at least here they might be able to lose their pursuers. They dropped into the maze of jetties, curving around the prow of a large frigate and ducking between a pair of dangling anchor-lines. But the endrinriggers were still coming, much faster and more manoeuvrable than the *Arbour Seed*. Another shot clipped the side of the sphere, and sparks flew.

'Hang on tight,' she shouted again. 'And secure the maps. I'm going to try something.'

She skimmed the top of a pontoon, startling a pair of drunken Duardin stumbling arm in arm. They gestured rudely, bellowing obscure curses. Then Alish twisted a dial and the ship tilted steeply downwards, plunging into the web of walkways. Everyone screamed, clinging on desperately as jetties flew by on either side in a blur of crazed movement. But the riggers were still after them, two of them closing fast.

One of them snatched for her and Alish scrabbled under the bench, swinging her hammer up and around, striking the Duardin square in the chest with a loud clang. He lost control of his endrin and spun wildly, slamming into a jetty.

But the other was still closing in, reaching for the airship's railing. Alish spun the wheel and the *Arbour Seed* slalomed sideways, swinging almost entirely around, missing a moored frigate by a whisker. She felt gravity tugging at her, throwing her one way then the other. Elio let out a shout and Kaspar laughed out loud. The endrinrigger was taken completely by surprise, crashing into a steel pontoon and tumbling into the foggy blackness below.

'Nice move!' Kiri shouted. 'Now get us out of here.'

'Wait!' Elio said, grabbing her arm. 'Where's Scratch?'

They looked around. The boy was gone.

'Did he jump out?' Thanis asked. 'Did he run away again?'

'There he is!' Alish pointed. He was dangling from a loose rope some

distance away, his face pale and his teeth chattering. 'He must've toppled out when we turned.'

A pair of endrinriggers closed in from either side, one reaching to grab hold of Scratch. He kicked and they broke off, circling back for another try. And more were on their way, though there was no longer any sign of Blackhammer.

Alish banked the ship, hitting the throttle.

'Are you sure

this is a good idea?' Elio asked. 'There are so many of them.'

'I won't leave anyone behind,' Alish said. 'Even him.'

They drew closer and Elio craned over the side, his legs held by Kiri and Thanis. The endrinriggers spiralled closer, lowering their pistols as the *Arbour Seed* banked and swerved, bullets glancing off the hull. Scratch saw the airship, his eyes widening as he reached out desperately. In that moment Alish remembered how young he was, and how far from any kind of home. His lip quivered, his face alight with hope.

Elio caught him, his hand locking around the boy's wrist. Scratch let go of the rope and swung down, thudding into the side of the *Arbour Seed*. Elio gave a cry as his arm was wrenched, but he managed to cling on as Alish swung them back towards the sky-port, bullets glancing off the sphere.

A tunnel opened up, a gaping mouth

ringed with walkways. They sped towards it, the hum of the endrin echoing as they shot inside. Kiri and Thanis hauled Elio back, and together they dragged Scratch over the side. He stood swaying, looking at them in amazement. *He thought we were going to leave him*, Alish realised.

Elio threw up his hands. 'Don't feel like you have to thank me or anything,' he said bitterly. 'I only risked my life to–'

Scratch threw himself forward, wrapping his arms around Elio and hugging him tight. Elio turned red, wriggling as Scratch buried his head in his chest. Then he reached down and patted the boy softly.

'There, there,' he said. 'It's over now.'

'No it isn't,' Kaspar said, and pointed.

The tunnel ran in a straight line through the middle of Barak-Mhornar, a central thoroughfare lined with stalls and storehouses. They were almost through; a short distance ahead they could see open sky and airships circling to land.

But beyond the entranceway Alish could see shapes circling towards them. The endrinriggers formed a defensive line, their pistols raised. And in the centre floated Blackhammer, his eyes bright with triumph, his pistol aimed right at them.

'Shut down your endrin,' he barked through a talking-horn. 'And give me my maps.'

## CHAPTER NINE

# Face-off

Alish slowed the airship as they drifted from the mouth of the tunnel, Blackhammer's henchmen closing in around them. The crimelord watched them through his goggles, raising the talking-horn to his lips.

'Foolish children,' he sneered. 'Did you really think you could rob me and get away with it? Now hand over my maps and I'll let you go.'

Kiri raised her catapult. 'They're not your maps, you stole them from Torvald Skysplitter. And now we've stolen them back from you.'

Blackhammer laughed. 'Torvald was

too blind to see what was happening under his fat red nose. Well, his shame is now complete. Using human children to do his dirty work, it's pathetic.'

He gestured to the endrinriggers and they drifted forward, closing on the *Arbour Seed*.

'Now I won't tell you again,' he said. 'Hand over the chest and you'll fly free. Refuse and you'll be sold to the cruellest master I can find.'

Kiri snarled, drawing back her catapult. But Kaspar put a hand on her arm.

'There are too many of them. I think we need to do as he says.'

'I think so too,' Thanis agreed. 'We can't fight them all.'

'But without the maps we'll never find Vertigan,' Alish protested.

'There'll be another way,' Elio said. 'There has to be.'

Kiri looked at their frightened faces then she sighed bitterly. 'I suppose our luck had to run out eventually. Thanis, help me lift this.'

Together they hefted the crate onto the *Arbour Seed*'s railing, holding it steady. Blackhammer's eyes gleamed and he started forward, holstering his pistol and reaching out hungrily.

Then a voice cried, 'Lower it! Now!'

Something dropped onto Blackhammer's shoulders: it was large and round and attached to a long pole, the steel ring tightening around his body. Alish looked up and saw the *Mercury Maid* powering in, three Duardin struggling to control the noose as Blackhammer fought to free himself. Torvald Skysplitter stood in the prow, laughing.

'This noose was built to hold a full-grown realm-rider,' he shouted. 'I think it can restrain one angry Kharadron, even one with a head as big as yours.'

Blackhammer writhed, his face purple with fury. He nodded to his endrinriggers. 'Get the maps! Now!'

They soared closer, descending on the *Arbour Seed*. Torvald looked down, assessing the situation.

'I'm truly grateful that you managed to rescue my property,' he told Alish and the others. 'But I'm afraid my friend here is a liar. Even if you give him the maps, his people won't let any of us go.'

'So what do we do?' Kiri shouted as the rigger swept in. 'We're trapped!'

Torvald nodded sadly. 'I'm afraid there's only one way to win.'

He raised his pistol and aimed it at the *Arbour Seed*.

Alish raised a hand in shock. 'No, what are you–'

But the bullet wasn't aimed at her, or the endrin, or the airship itself. Instead it struck the wooden chest, exploding the lock into fragments. The lid flew open – inside the scrolls lay stacked on top of one another, rustling as the wind blew.

'It's like you said,' Torvald shouted. 'I

can always make more. Lives are more important than pieces of paper.'

Blackhammer wrestled with the noose. One of his endrinriggers was wielding a serrated knife in an effort to cut his master loose. 'Don't you dare!' the big Duardin roared. 'You give those maps back!'

Kiri looked down at the chest, shaking her head. Thanis reached out and took her hand.

'We'll find Vertigan another way. And we'll never find him at all if Blackhammer's men get hold of us.'

Kiri sighed and nodded, and together they gave a shove.

The chest toppled over the side of the *Arbour Seed* and out into open air. It spun as it fell, the maps flying free and fluttering on the breeze.

Blackhammer broke from the noose and raised his talking-horn, pointing frantically downwards. 'Forget the children,' he cried to his men. 'Get the maps!'

The endrinriggers broke off their advance, dropping rapidly. But the maps were falling faster, flapping away into the black clouds. A few dropped onto jetties and airships, where Duardin picked them up and inspected them.

'Legitimate salvage,' Kaspar laughed.

The *Mercury Maid*'s prow drew level with the *Arbour Seed*, and they turned to see Torvald waving from the deck.

'You should get out of here while you can. I'll keep Blackhammer busy.'

'What about your maps?' Kiri asked. 'Your family's legacy?'

'Pieces of paper,' Torvald said with a wave of his hand. 'Like you said, I'm a born cartographer, I can start again from scratch. Blackhammer can't.'

'Thank you,' Alish said. 'For everything. I'll never forget all this.' She gestured to the sky-port and the Ironclad, and the endrinriggers soaring through the clouds.

Torvald smiled. 'Keep inventing,' he said. 'One day I expect to call you captain.'

Alish opened the regulator, and the *Arbour Seed* shot away into the dark.

Dawn found them soaring over a silver sea, the clouds breaking as the pale sun rose. Alish stood in the prow, her hand on the tiller. The others huddled in the back, Thanis and Scratch snoring side by side while the rest tried to figure out what they were supposed to do now. In the hours since they'd escaped from Barak-Mhornar their joy had turned to doubt, their relief at escaping Blackhammer's clutches eaten away by the realisation that they were in a strange realm, lost and alone, with no idea how to get home.

'Torvald told us not all of the sky-ports were so dangerous,' Elio was saying. 'If we could reach one of the safer ones maybe somebody will help us.'

'But how do we find them?' Kiri asked. 'We have no idea where we are. We haven't even seen any land, let alone any towns. Just this endless ocean.'

'And the aether-gold won't last forever,' Alish said. 'We've already used most of what Torvald gave us, and it wasn't much to begin with. I suppose we could look for more but I don't really know how they harvest it, it's supposed to be refined or something before you can put it in the endrin.'

'So should we turn around?' Kaspar asked. 'This ocean could take days to cross and I'm not even sure it's made of water, I think it might be some kind of molten metal. If we were forced to land in it we might float or sink or just burn to cinders.'

Kiri shot him a dark look. 'There's no need for talk like that,' she said.

There was a sudden thud, and the airship's timbers shook.

Thanis and Scratch woke, jumping to their feet. Something had appeared on the starboard side, a steel hook biting into the wood. The *Arbour Seed* rocked violently, tipping so hard that Elio staggered, grabbing the railing. Alish peered over the side. What she saw was both incredible and frightening.

There was a boat down there, a steel-sided vessel adrift in the sparkling sea. The hook had been fired from a giant crossbow on the deck – there was a rope dangling from it, tied to a winch operated by a number of small, scurrying figures.

'Are those...' Elio said, scratching his head. 'Are those *Skaven*?'

'Kreech,' Kiri said through tight lips. Then she grabbed Scratch by his jacket. 'How did he find us?' she demanded, but the boy just stared up at her, eyes wide and fearful.

The rope tightened and the airship

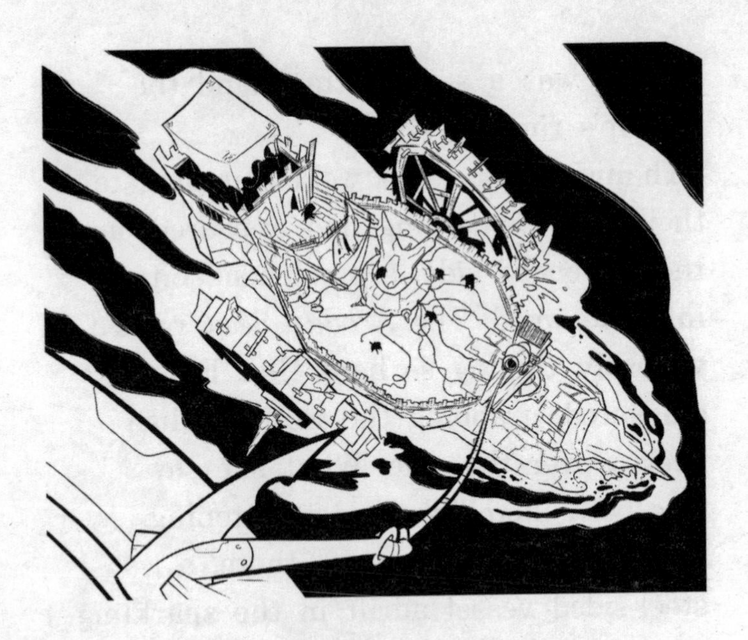

tipped again, forcing them to cling on. Alish could feel the *Arbour Seed* descending, the rope jerking as the Skaven worked the winch, hauling them like a hooked fish right out of the sky.

## CHAPTER TEN

# The Black Ship

Kiri snatched up a piece of jagged metal from the floor of the airship. 'We could cut the rope,' she said. 'We could get out of here.'

'But then we'd be back where we were before,' Kaspar said. 'At least this way we know we'll live at least one more day.'

'One more day among the Skaven,' Thanis snarled. 'I hate those rats.'

Another hook whistled out of the air, latching onto the port side. Now they were truly trapped, the airship descending rapidly. Looking over the edge they could see a figure emerging from the cabin and striding across the deck. Alish recognised him right away – the packlord Kreech, resplendent in a purple robe. He raised a hand, and exposed his foul pointed teeth as he grinned victoriously at them.

'Little man-things!' he called up as the winches groaned, the boat drawing closer. 'How good-good to see you again. And my beloved pet, too!'

Scratch watched his master with dark eyes, and as they bumped onto the deck he clutched Alish's hand.

'Come out, all of you,' Kreech said, sweeping his robe back. 'You won't be fly-flying any further today, no-no.'

They did as they were told, climbing onto the deck. Kreech's ship was constructed entirely of steel, the hull and the mast and the cabin. Even the ropes were more like twisted cables, the sails made from fine, beaten metal.

'How did you know where to find us?' Kiri asked, facing the Skaven as he smiled from ear to pointed ear, clasping his claws together. All around them other ratmen were drawing in, bobbing their furry heads.

'Why, she told me of course,' Kreech said. 'The one we all-all serve. Ashnakh, the great-great sorceress.'

'She's here?' Elio asked, looking around fearfully.

Kreech shook his head. 'No-no. But I can speak to her. Using this.'

He reached down, pulling something from his pocket and opening his palm. An object lay there, sparkling in the pale sun. It was black, and small.

And shaped like a pyramid.

Alish heard herself gasp. Slowly they turned – Kiri then Thanis, Elio then Alish – all of them staring directly at Kaspar. He opened his mouth, then he shut it again.

'How did Ashnakh know where we were?' Kiri asked, forcing the words out. 'How did she even know which realm we were in?'

'I...' Kaspar started. 'You don't...'

'Tell us,' Thanis said, her face turning red. 'Tell us this isn't how it looks. Please, Kaspar, tell us!'

He swallowed hard, taking the identical pyramid from around his neck and holding it up. 'You don't understand. You don't know how powerful she is. She speaks to me, inside my head, through this. She's been ahead of us all along. Our only hope is to do as she asks, and maybe she'll let us keep our lives.'

'No!' Thanis screamed and suddenly

she was launching at him, dropping the staff and grabbing him by the throat, squeezing hard. 'You coward, you traitor!'

Kaspar spluttered, gripping her hands in a desperate attempt to prise himself loose. But Thanis was too strong. Tears were coursing down her face.

'I thought I could trust you,' she moaned. 'I thought you were my friend.'

Kiri glanced at Elio and together they took hold of Thanis, pulling her back as gently as they could. She didn't even fight, just turned away tearfully as Kaspar dropped to the floor, coughing and gasping.

Kreech laughed, a thin, cackling sound. 'Oh, poor-poor little creatures,' he said. 'You've tried so hard, but now it's all over. Kreech has you in his power, six little man-things with six little marks, and he's going to make her pay-pay. Oh yes.'

'You're a fool.' Kaspar lifted his head, staring at Kreech and rubbing his throat. 'You can't trick her. She knows everything, she has eyes everywhere. She'll turn you inside out and use your guts to string her bow.'

Kreech blanched. 'She'll have to find-find me first.'

Kaspar struggled to his feet. 'Believe me, she already has. It's just a matter of–'

The sound came from nowhere, a deep rolling boom that echoed over the ocean. The steel ship vibrated with the force of it, every bolt rattling.

'Time,' Kaspar finished, and Kreech looked up in horror.

A huge shape was emerging from the fog, dark against the silvery mist. It was a vast ship, its wooden timbers so deeply black they were almost hard to see, as though a ship-shaped hole had been cut into the realm itself.

Alish saw a tall mast with sails hanging limply from it. Figures scaled the rigging, ragged clothes hanging from dry bones. Others clustered at the railing, looking down with blank, eyeless faces. Deadwalkers.

Then another sound rose – a hissing and whispering, growing steadily in volume. Something rose from the deck, drifting towards the prow and over it. Alish saw spectral forms weaving and spiralling in mid-air, a formless mass of crackling energy and purple-edged darkness. And within it she could make out a figure, her hands outstretched as she floated down towards them, landing lightly on the steel ship.

The Skaven sailors dropped to their knees, bowing and scraping. Kreech lowered his head as the spectral shapes withdrew, revealing the sorceress's pale, perfect, faintly smiling face.

'M-mistress,' the packlord managed, his voice quaking with terror. 'I'm so glad-glad you're here. Look, I have all the man-thing children you w–'

Ashnakh made a gesture and his voice caught in his throat, his whole body contorting. His claws contracted and his breath turned to a hiss, his eyes bulging from their sockets.

'I don't need to listen to your lies any longer, treacherous rat-thing,' the sorceress said. 'Kaspar told me about the seventh mark, that you were hiding him all this time. I came to your warren, but you were already gone, along with your pet.'

She smiled at Scratch but he just stared back, shaking with fear. Kreech reached out desperately; the ends of his fur were turning grey, as though Ashnakh's spell was ageing him prematurely.

'I was keeping him safe,' he croaked. 'For you... mistress. Only... for... you.'

He fell to the floor, his body wracked with shudders. Ashnakh looked at Kaspar.

'At least you never betrayed me, brave boy. Thank you for leading me to this creature. And to your friends.'

Thanis sobbed, looking away. Kaspar's face was an emotionless mask.

'You see?' he said. 'We couldn't run. We couldn't hide. I didn't have a choice.'

'He's right,' Ashnakh said. 'And now you're coming with me.'

She waved a hand and a pale mist rose from the black ship, coiling towards them. Alish saw twisted shapes inside it, their arms outstretched as they descended towards the children. Kiri raised her catapult and Thanis seized her staff, the two of them locking arms. Elio joined them and Alish reached out too, feeling the strength in her veins. Then a thought struck her and she reached for Scratch, beckoning.

'Join us,' she said. 'Come on!'

But the boy wasn't looking at her. His eyes were fixed on the sorceress and her spectral servants, his face a mask. He whined, a low sound of absolute terror.

Then suddenly he broke, fleeing across the deck. He darted past a pair of kneeling Skaven, throwing a panicked glance back as he ran.

'Go after him,' Ashnakh told Kaspar, and he nodded briskly.

'Of course, mistress.'

Scratch had reached the steel ship's railing, peering fearfully over the side. Kaspar ran after him, spreading his arms to cut off the boy's escape. Scratch tried to dart left but Kaspar was there ahead of him, shaking his head. Alish saw his lips move but they were too far away, she couldn't hear what Kaspar was saying. Scratch stared up at him, his blue eyes wide with fear and disbelief.

Then he backed to the railing, pulled himself over and jumped from the ship.

Alish felt her heart seize. Thanis gave a cry, Kiri started forward. Kaspar looked down, reaching over the side of the ship. Then they saw him turn back, his face dark. Slowly, he shook his head.

'I tried to stop him,' Kaspar told

the sorceress as she strode forward, stepping over Kreech's contorted form. 'He was too scared. He jumped straight into the ocean. It's pure mercury, there's no way he could have survived.'

Alish heard herself cry out, but it was drowned by the howl that rose from Ashnakh's throat, a searing screech of absolute fury and horror.

'No!' she screamed. 'No, it can't be. He was the seventh mark – without him the ritual is impossible, without him this has all been for nothing!'

She clawed at her face in anger and frustration, leaving red marks on her perfect white skin. The spirits weaved in the air above her head, as though afraid to come too near. Alish sobbed, and Thanis held her close. Kaspar stood apart from them, watching silently.

Then Ashnakh turned back, forcing herself back under control. 'This is just a setback,' she said through gritted teeth. 'I still have all of you, this simply means that things will take a little longer than I had planned. Another mark will be called – it could take years, but it will happen.'

'Y-years?' Kiri managed. 'But what does… What will…?'

'What will I do with you?' Ashnakh sneered. 'Until then you will all be my guests in the realm of Shyish. Trapped, like your master, in my Castle of Mirrors.'

# REALMS ARCANA

## PART FOUR

### THE MORTAL REALMS

Each of the Mortal Realms is a world unto itself, steeped in powerful magic. Seemingly infinite in size, they contain limitless possibilities for discovery and adventure: floating cities and enchanted woodlands, noble beings and dread beasts beyond imagination. But in every corner of every realm, a war rages between the armies of Order and the forces of Chaos. This centuries-long conflict must be won if the realms are to live in peace and freedom.

**AZYR**

The Realm of Heavens, where the immortal King Sigmar reigns unchallenged.

**AQSHY**

The Realm of Fire, a region of mighty volcanoes, molten seas and flaming-hot tempers.

**GHYRAN**

The Realm of Life, where flourishing forests teem with creatures beyond counting.

**CHAMON**

The Realm of Metal, where rivers of mercury flow through canyons of steel.

**SHYISH**

The Realm of Death, a lifeless land where spirits drift through silent, shaded tombs.

**GHUR**

The Realm of Beasts, where living monstrosities battle for dominance.

**HYSH**

The Realm of Light, where knowledge and wisdom are prized above all.

**ULGU**

The Realm of Shadows, a domain of darkness where dread phantoms lurk.

## KHARADRON OVERLORDS

This remarkable race of Duardin dwarf-folk have discovered the secret of manned flight. Powered by the mysterious substance aether-gold (see below), the Kharadron's mighty airships ply trade routes throughout the Mortal Realms, though they are most populous in Chamon, the Realm of Metal. From vast Ironclads and nimble Gunhaulers to one-man 'endrin rigs',

the Kharadron fleets are a wonder to behold – and they are greatly feared in battle.

## AETHER-GOLD

The mystical element that powers the airships and flying fortresses of the Kharadron Overlords, aether-gold is one of the most highly prized commodities in the Mortal Realms. It's mined from the clouds above Chamon and other realms, appearing as shimmering seams woven through the air. Having been refined by Duardin aether-khemists, the substance is then fed into the huge spherical aether-endrins that keep the airships aloft.

## CHAMON

Named the Realm of Metal, Chamon is rich in minerals beyond counting. Trees of bronze grow on slopes of iron ore, while oceans of molten gold lap on shores of burnished steel. The realm is a natural home for the Duardin – builders and traders in mechanical artefacts, weapons and machines. Notable regions of Chamon include the Hanging Valleys, mountainous floating islands joined by rivers of silver, and the Iron Mountains, where the Duardin's lord of blacksmiths, Grungni,

was freed from his chains by the immortal King Sigmar.

## SKY-PORTS

In addition to their mighty airships, the Kharadron Overlords have also fashioned enormous sky-ports, floating cities in the skies above Chamon. Teeming with Duardin traders, soldiers and craftsmen, these vast metropolises lie close to vital sources of aether-gold, the mineral that keeps them aloft. Important sky-ports include Barak-Urbaz, the bustling Market City; Barak-Thryng, the noble City of the Ancestors; and Barak-Mhornar, the dark and perilous City of Shadow.

## ALISH

Bearing the mark of Hysh, the Realm of Light, eleven-year-old orphan Alish is restless, inquisitive and highly intelligent, with the instinctive ability to understand and repair almost any mechanical device. But her true passion is for inventing: in her workshop she has designed and built countless contraptions, from clocks and counting machines to a full-sized airship named the *Arbour Seed*. The one thing Alish won't make any more is weapons: she prefers a creative solution to any conflict.

## THE SCARLET SHADOW

Before she met her friends and became part of Vertigan's group at the Arbour, Alish was a prisoner of the Scarlet Shadow, one of the most feared gangs in the city of Lifestone. They forced her to craft weapons for them – crossbows, swords and explosives – exploiting her natural ability to suit their own cruel ends. Run by the mysterious Stonejaw, the Shadow are just one of many criminal gangs that have flourished in Lifestone in recent years, making a living by preying on the local populace.

## TORVALD SKYSPLITTER

A Duardin from a family of respected Kharadron cartographers, Torvald Skysplitter is the captain of a small fleet of flying machines who trade and barter in the skies above Chamon. Raised to be a mapmaker like his ancestors before him, Torvald lost his family fortune when he allowed a young midshipman named Blackhammer to make off with his precious maps. Now he's been reduced to menial work like trading machine parts and gold, and the bile of a wingless realm-rider. Loud, boisterous and short-tempered, Torvald Skysplitter nevertheless has a good heart.

## WINGLESS REALM-RIDER

One of many flying beasts that soar the skies of Chamon, the wingless realm-rider is a distant cousin to the shark-like megalofin that plague the fleets of the Kharadron. Held aloft by the aether-gold it ingests as it flies, the realm-rider has the rare ability to pass from one realm to another, feeding in Chamon but spawning in Ghyran, the Realm of Life, where its young have a better chance of survival.

## BLACKHAMMER

A ruthless Kharadron crimelord who'll stop at nothing to get what he wants, Arkanaut Admiral Blackhammer is the most powerful Duardin in the sky-port of Barak-Mhornar, the City of Shadow. Working his way up through the ranks until he was hired as a midshipman under Captain Torvald Skysplitter, Blackhammer's fortunes changed overnight when he robbed Torvald of his maps and went into business for himself. He has since acquired vast riches, storing all his wealth aboard his huge Ironclad airship, the *Hammerhead*, where it is guarded day and night by platoons of armed Kharadron.

## ABOUT THE AUTHOR

**Tom Huddleston** is the author of the *Warhammer Adventures: Realm Quest* series, and has also written three instalments in the *Star Wars: Adventures in Wild Space* saga. His other works include the futuristic fantasy adventure story *FloodWorld* and its upcoming sequel, *DustRoad*. He lives in East London, and you can find him online at www.tomhuddleston.co.uk.

## ABOUT THE ARTISTS

**Dan Boultwood** is a comic book artist and illustrator from London. When he's not drawing, he collects old shellac records and dances around badly to them in between taking forever to paint his miniatures.

**Cole Marchetti** is an illustrator and concept artist from California. When he isn't sitting in front of the computer, he enjoys hiking and plein air painting. Warhammer Adventures is his first project working with Games Workshop.

**An Extract from book five**
***Fortress of Ghosts***
**by Tom Huddleston**
(out November 2020)

As the sun sank, the seas of Shyish turned red as blood.

Kaspar stood on the quarterdeck of the huge black ship, staring out across the rolling waves. Dark shapes moved beneath the water, tentacles coiled to the surface and sank from sight, nested eyes glinting in the depths. Something large brushed against the side of the ship; he felt the deck tremble with the force of it.

On the outer rigging one of the

deadwalker sailors lost his footing, bony fingers snatching at the ropes as he fell. He landed on his back in the water, empty eye sockets staring up. Then a dark form rose, black teeth bared in a rotted grey maw, a tattered fin hanging limply in the red light. The dead shark took the sailor in its gaping jaws, and Kaspar heard the crack of bones.

He turned away, his stomach roiling. They'd reached the Realm of Death three days earlier, passing through a Realmgate shaped like a giant water-tornado, which had swirled the ship and its crew up into the glittering skies of Chamon and dropped them with a splash into the Sea of Fading Hope, one of the vast oceans of Shyish.

Kaspar had felt queasy ever since, and not just from seasickness. The air felt heavy somehow, clammy and oppressive. The presence of all these walking corpses disgusted him; their rotting frames and bony hands, their grinning, empty skulls. Even the pyramid around his neck seemed to have grown heavier, its dragging weight reminding him of all the choices he'd made to get here.

But at least he could breathe free. Down on the main deck a large wooden crate stood lashed with rope. There were small holes in the top but no windows, no bars. His companions had been locked inside since Ashnakh had captured them, and he could only imagine how they'd been suffering. They'd survive, they were strong, but it must be miserable in there.

'You don't have to worry about them any more,' Ashnakh said, and Kaspar started. She'd have made a good thief, he thought; she moved even more softly than he did. Perhaps it had something to do with being undead. 'They made their choice. They chose to defy me and now they're paying the price. We all are.' She sighed bitterly.

'I tried to stop Scratch from jumping,' Kaspar said. 'I failed you, mistress.'

'That foolish, frightened child,' the sorceress snarled. 'How could he have been so reckless? And now all my work is ruined, all my plans come to nothing. All we can do is wait until another is called. Still, my lord is nothing if not patient.'

Kaspar shuddered. Ashnakh was doing all of this for her master, Nagash, the Lord of Death. It was for him that she'd tracked down the six marked children, luring them with the promise of finding their own mentor, Vertigan. But she'd pushed too hard and one of them had snapped; the feral boy known as Scratch had leapt over the railing of the ship, shocking them all. Now Ashnakh was determined to keep the rest of them imprisoned until another marked child was called, even if it took years.

The sun dipped below the horizon

and in the stillness Kaspar heard the splash and slither of a million slimy things. A flock of ragged birds passed over, oily feathers clinging to their skeletal pinions, their hoarse moans echoing over the water. But they soared too low and a huge rotting tongue uncoiled from the ocean, lashing around one of the birds and dragging it, screeching, from the sky.

Then he saw a flash of light and raised his head. Ahead of them a vast shape rose from the water – a stony island, large and dark, hunched like a sleeping troggoth over the black sea. Pale mists gathered on its shores and in the depths he saw that light again, a golden flare glancing through the fog.

'Is it a lighthouse?' he asked. He'd read about them in a story once.

Ashnakh shook her head. 'That is your new home. My Castle of Mirrors.'

She made a gesture and the fog banks parted, rolling back over the rugged rocks. On the clifftops a great spire was revealed, a tower so tall that its upper levels were still in sunlight, sending shafts of red light across the churning sea. But why were the light-beams moving? Kaspar shielded his eyes, took a closer look, and finally understood.

The Castle of Mirrors was aptly named – every part of it was constructed from vast sheets of glass, each one bigger than the last. But somehow they were floating free, unconnected to one another, the entire structure slowly revolving. As they moved the mirrors caught the sun's last radiance, casting it out into the evening air in a glancing dance of ghostly light.

He gripped the railing, remembering the vision Ashnakh had shown him, that night at the Arbour. The castle was terrifying but it was beautiful too, a sight more majestic than any he'd seen. He could barely imagine stepping inside it, but a part of him couldn't wait to.

He heard the crash of waves and the creak of timbers, and as they drew closer to the island he saw the wrecks of sunken ships on either side, broken prows jutting from the water. A figurehead rose, sculpted like a warrior woman, but so rotten now that her eyes were black holes, her mouth a twisted grimace.

The corpse sailors worked the ropes, lowering the sails with a snap and a creak. One of them got his foot caught, and tried desperately to pull himself free as he was dragged towards a spinning winch. But it was too late; the rope snapped as the deadwalker flew to pieces, his skull skittering across the deck.

Then there was a thump, and the ship stopped dead. Peering over the railing Kaspar saw a stone pier clinging to the cliff face. Ropes dropped from the side of the ship, lashed to the jetty by gangs of skeletal dock-workers. They had arrived.

On the deck he saw deadwalkers swarming all over the wooden crate, tying ropes and tightening chains. It rose into the air, lifted by a large crane-arm that swung out over the dock. Kaspar heard a muffled cry and turned away.

'Come,' Ashnakh said, taking his arm. They descended the gangplank, Kaspar's stomach turning as he touched solid ground. Above him he saw the crate swinging off the dock, being lowered onto a wooden cart.

Ashnakh raised her hands, weaving them in the air and whispering soft words. Against the cliff wall Kaspar saw a pile of white fragments. He'd thought they were pale pieces of stone, but now they began to rise, floating and spinning. They were bones, he realised, legs and ribs and skulls, all coming together to form a pair of large, four-legged shapes, their heads bowed as they faced Ashnakh.

She clicked her tongue and the skeletal horses stepped forward, their hooves clopping on the stone jetty. One approached Kaspar, lowering its fleshless snout. A saddle was placed on its back and Ashnakh gestured, mounting her own steed. 'It won't bite,' she said. 'Unless I want it to.'

Kaspar looked into the horse's empty eye socket and tried to understand. Did the creature know what it was, or if it was? Was there a mind in there, or a soul? Might this be his fate some day, to be a corpse enslaved to Ashnakh, trapped inside his rotting body, unable to think for himself?

Shivering, he took hold of the bridle, hoisting himself up. Ashnakh's horse advanced and Kaspar followed, looking down through the creature's undulating ribcage to the stones beneath. A whip cracked and the cart drew in behind them, pulled by a line of straining deadwalkers.

A path wound across the cliff, just wide enough for the cart and its unsteady burden. Light shimmered below and Kaspar realised that the track was made from fragments of shattered glass, reflecting the light of the rising moon. Then they reached the top, and he looked out over the scorched landscape of the island.

'Its name is the Battlerock,' Ashnakh said. 'And it is my dominion.'

In the far distance the ground rose, a bare ridge crossing the centre of the island. To Kaspar's left the Castle of Mirrors stood tall on the cliff edge, dark panes circling. All around it lay a dense layer of mist, hugging the foot of the tower and coiling outwards in every direction. The path led towards it, vanishing into the gloom.

'Stay close, and do not stray,' Ashnakh told Kaspar as they approached the fog bank. Tendrils of vapour coiled around the horses' hooves. 'This is no ordinary mist. We are entering the Shatterglass Labyrinth, there are spells here to confuse the mind and baffle the senses. If you lose yourself, even I might not be able to find you again.'

Shapes rose on either side, dark walls closing them in. But these were not stone barricades, Kaspar saw – they were formed from shards of broken glass, huge fractured panes reflecting the moon, and the mist, and each other. The track split and split again, countless small ways branching from the wider path. But Ashnakh held her course, her undead steed moving slowly, purposefully through the fog.

Kaspar shivered, imagining what it would be like to lose yourself in that pale, drifting emptiness. Then he heard a sound and turned sharply. It was a shout, or many shouts, muffled by the mist. It came again and he heard the clash of swords, and the fearful whinnying of horses. In the mirrors he saw movement – the spectral forms of warriors, almost lost in the shadows.

'The Battlerock is aptly named,' Ashnakh told him. 'There was a mighty conflict here once, and its echoes still remain. Two vast armies came together, fighting so long and so hard that when they were done nothing was left alive, not an insect, not a shrub, not a blade of grass. And so it remains, centuries later. This is a dead place.'

'But why here?' Kaspar asked. 'Why fight over this lump of rock?'

'Because of that,' Ashnakh said, pointing between the mirrored walls, above the shifting fog, towards the centre of the island. At first Kaspar could see nothing, just the stony ridge lifting towards the clouds. But then he saw a purple shimmer in the air above it, rising from the dark stones.

'A Realmgate,' he said. 'The one that

links to Rawdeep Mere!'

Ashnakh smiled. 'Clever boy. This island is of huge strategic importance, that is why my lord Nagash entrusted it to me. And he gave me a purpose, too. A prize to win, a city to claim. My home.'

'Lifestone,' Kaspar said. 'This is where your army marched from.'

'It is,' Ashnaskh nodded. 'And very soon, you will understand why.'

She tugged on the reins and the skeletal steed halted, the cart grinding to a stop behind them. One of the undead hauliers took out a crowbar, plunging it into a crack in the side of the crate. He heaved and the side wall worked loose, dropping with a crash. For a long moment there was silence. Kaspar felt his heart pound.

Then Thanis and Kiri jumped down together, arms linked as they hit the ground. They looked at the mist surrounding them, the mirrored walls rising, the deadwalkers standing in dumb silence. Then they saw Ashnakh and Kaspar, and Thanis's eyes flashed with loathing.

'So this is Shyish,' Alish said, clambering down behind them.

Elio followed, shivering. 'It's pretty much what I expected. Cold, dreary.'

'And full of evil things,' Thanis added, her eyes still on Kaspar.

Ashnakh snorted. 'Look around you, children. The Battlerock is a place of wonders. Witness, my Castle of Mirrors.'

They peered up at the great tower, shimmering in the moonlight. Alish's mouth fell open but she shut it again quickly.

'Personally,' she said, 'I preferred the Kharadron sky-city.'

'Or the Elmheart Glade,' Elio agreed. 'That was much more impressive.'

'Silence!' Ashnakh snapped. 'You are in the heart of the Shatterglass Labyrinth, a place from which there is no escape. Here you will wait until I have need of you again.'

Kiri looked around, then back up at Ashnakh. 'So you want us to just wander about? That doesn't sound so bad.'

Ashnakh smiled, waving a hand. 'Yes, be my guest. Roam. Explore. Lose yourselves in the labyrinth. There is no way out, though I know that won't stop you from searching. Oh, but you should know one thing. You're not alone.'

She coiled her fingers and the mist shifted around them, swirling upwards from the ground, forming dark and nebulous shapes. Kaspar felt a chill in his bones, a heaviness in his heart. He heard a wail and the rattle of chains.

'My nighthaunts,' Ashnakh whispered. 'Beautiful, aren't they?'

Spectral shapes emerged from the mist like something from the deepest nightmare. They were hooded figures, with long, bony arms and skull-like faces. Each was wrapped in clanking chains, and some also carried weapons – notched swords, rusted daggers and long-bladed scythes.

Thanis gritted her teeth. 'You won't let them kill us,' she said. 'You need us alive to perform this ritual of yours.'

Ashnakh's smile broadened. 'No, they won't kill you,' she admitted as the spectres closed in. 'But of course, murder is not a chainghast's specialty.'

'Wh... what is?' Alish asked as the rattling grew louder.

Ashnakh chuckled, and slowly her head turned. Kaspar looked up in surprise as her eyes fixed directly on his.

'Fear,' she said. 'Fear is how I will control you.'

He felt a chill on his back, a shiver rising. Tearing his eyes from Ashnakh he looked over his shoulder and cried out in shock.

The nighthaunt had approached so

silently that he hadn't noticed it; now it was almost upon him, its rictus mouth open in silent laughter, its bone-fingered hands weaving as it came. The terror that gripped Kaspar was more intense than anything he'd ever felt; he could barely move, barely speak, waves of fear coursing like cold mercury through his veins.

'Mistress, no,' he managed. 'Haven't I done everything you asked of me? Haven't I been faithful to you?'

Ashnakh snorted softly. 'Of course you have, dear Kaspar. But one can never be too careful.'

The apparition reached out, and the last thing Kaspar heard before the darkness overcame him was his own voice, desperately shrieking.